The Pendulum of Magic series:

Book 1:   *The Renewal | MAGIC*

Book 2:   *All the Stories | MAGIC*

Book 3:   *The Book of Words | MAGIC*

And a compendium ...
Book 4:   *all the words | MAGIC*

Visit the author page on Amazon: **Dominic Wharram**

The Renewal | MAGIC

Dominic Wharram
dCoached LLC
PUBLISHING arm

Reviews so far ...

The Renewal | MAGIC – Book 1 reactions:

"...definitely something different. Looking forward to book 2!" ~Sam T.

"Can't wait for book 2!!" ~Jen W.

"Nice nod to Arthurian legend. Good story!" ~Matt W.

"Magic: Time, cool things, modern castle, great characters. All the right stuff!" ~Tom B.

All the Stories | MAGIC – Book 2 early reactions (pre-publishing):

"A little headier about the human condition if you that's what people like (I do) and every bit as entertaining as a book about magic should be! Keep it up ... looking forward to book 3 now as well as re-reading book 1. I'm sure I missed some things!" ~Mark S.

"WOW. The characters get better and better. The stories are surprisingly fresh. Very enjoyable quick read." ~Tim B.

"Very cool flow. Fun to read. Great new view of magic and the history. It almost makes me think this is a real story" ~Patricia I.

"I can see this on Netflix or HBO for sure! Find an agent. I'd watch it." ~Samantha H.

"New magic origin stories, with a twist. Love it!" ~Anonymous submission via website

Publisher:

dCoached LLC
Publishing arm
909 County Road 19
Independence, MN. 55359

ISBN: 978-1-886084-00-1 (digital)
ISBN: 978-1-886084-01-8 (paperback) V.0823
ISBN: 978-1-886084-02-5 (hardcover)

Contact Author for sealed 8.5X11 personally printed &
sealed manuscript

Table of Contents

Before Maddison						Maddison in the study	The Renewal				
1 & 2	3	4	5	6	7	8 – 9 – 10	11	12	13	14	15
450 AD	1955	1980	2004	2016	2017	2018	2019 Early	2019 Midyear	2019 Late	2020 Early	2020 Midyear

The Renewal | MAGIC
Book 1

Before Maddison...

Scene 1 | Poof

The year is 450

There is clearly magic in the room. Not *dark magic* or *black magic*. Not even *good* magic or bad, for that matter. It's a feeling. We all 'feel' something from time to time when we enter certain places. There was a fire. There was a cauldron. And there was a black cat roaming about. There was also a woman, the widow. She was simply looking around, trying to imagine how all the others were seeing things for the first time since none of them had been there before.

The room was cathedral-like in size and space but had the pleasant, faint smell of a metalsmith's shop mixed with smoke from burning a pleasant sap in the fall. But she noted that the smell didn't match what everyone would be looking at. The room had perfectly smooth stone floors that were not slippery, and walls crafted with artful mixtures of natural stone and wood, as well as uniquely placed fired bricks. There was wooden furniture that seemed to be in proper arrangement in various areas of the giant room. There were vines meandering up the great walls. Although none of it matched, all of it seemed to go together perfectly, she thought. There was plenty of light streaming in, and there were plants of all sorts in one whole corner of the cathedral space. It looked like a sort of green house without the glass walls. And the vines shot all the way to the timbers and then dangled down a little. The effect was very dramatic, and yet the air wasn't damp.

Folks were entering and engaging. Everything in the room seemed to be working in harmony, creating real warmth and an inviting feeling despite the grand hall's size. Looking around, the room should have been intimidating and awesome, but it didn't feel that way. It felt magical in plenty of ways. Everyone else seemed to feel that too as she continued watching from the side.

She knew everyone in the room had been asked to be there. She heard some call him Teacher. She heard laughter popping up from time to time. She heard raised voices, but not anger. Everyone was inching closer to the curious stone table in front of the cauldron.

She had never met these people, and she found it interesting the collection of folks the Teacher had gathered for this work—the work of renewing magic. The work she and her Husband were going to handle themselves, but now... well, now she was looking at the people who were dedicating their lives to this work. Amazing group of people, she finally concluded as she looked at them: Odd, disjointed, and the room seemed calm as the Teacher made his way through the group to the fire.

Some were well dressed, and some were in plain clothes. Some had massive swords and shields displayed by the doorway, while others carried tattered baskets containing what appeared to be rabbit skins or cloth-wrapped bread. Some had hats, and some had their hair tied back with pieces of cloth.

She saw his face change from smiling to one without that smile, which was dramatic. He was changing from warm to serious, intense, commanding, and yet trustworthy.

She heard him clear his throat and turn from the folks with whom he was chatting. He took a breath—something that sounded like a great sigh, or maybe a deep breath before a race, maybe mixed with what it sounds like to draw in the aroma of fresh baked bread. He'd silenced the room, however it sounded to each.

She watched as the Teacher approached the table, taking a mental note of the carving on the table, the fire, and the cauldron just behind it. The goblet he held had a special spot on the table. He double-checked that the quill and ink were in order. She knew he was taking a quick and final inventory to be sure all was set.

He slowed his approach, just short of stumbling. The cat around his feet required him to do so. His smile crossed his face, fleetingly, as he watched his cat move along and out of the way.

She alone noticed he had slowed for the cat to carry on, and it made her smile as well. She looked down to be sure no one saw her face right then. Everyone thought she was a maid of the house or something along those lines, ignoring her for the most part.

The Teacher set his goblet where it was supposed to be on the interesting table and looked up at everyone who was silent and ready. Whatever *ready* meant.

"Well, friends," he began, pausing only long enough to add some emphasis to the rest of his opening remarks: "And I know some of you are foes as well. Here we are, and I want to thank you." And that's how he started. It was a powerful voice—one not heard by this audience before—yet all of them had spent many hours with him individually preparing for this day and getting to know him a little more. It was clear to her that everyone was paying attention. And so he continued:

"We are placing trust in one another. Each of you trusts me, knowing that I will do as I say. I trust that you will do your part diligently. We are all so inextricably linked as a chain that none of us can break it. That's the trust we are placing in each other today. And I do it with great confidence. My hope is that each of you is doing so willingly."

He continued. "I've spoken to each of you about your task. We've designed your scroll to be very clear about what you're about to set your heart to and what you'll get in return. So, we all hear it the same way: we are counting on one another. I am counting on you. If we don't succeed, and there will be times where we, each, will question ourselves and the decision we make today, all will be for naught."

She knew he paused to let that settle in. But she could also tell that even he didn't think it sounded strong enough. He continued...

He turned from the curious table toward the fire and cauldron.

"After all. Renewing magic is no small feat." And with that, the fire was stoked, and his voice seemed to grow in a way that filled the room.

"As you are aware, time works both for and against us. Your task, once you begin, will take you to the time and place where you will be best suited to stop the magic causing so much pain and return to me whatever magical gift was given that is now being abused. This will take only a moment—or a lifetime. In either case, it will be up to you at that point to take it on or walk away. I will be waiting right here for either outcome. Bring what you've gathered to me, and you can live free in the life you'll have then, or you can fly into the world as an eagle, safe for the duration of your life. The way I understand this, we may be consumed and tired after our task. The escape of flying away and being tended to might be exactly what one needs. Or, it may enliven us, and continuing on for more may be our desire. Each of you will learn which is best in the end."

"To be sure, as of today, we all walk away from our current lives. We leave this room today with our medallion." He said.

He continued, "Accepting our role as the ones who will give the final push to the pendulum, required to renew the gift of magic. This medallion represents our hope of magic being renewed for all the wonders of the world to be enjoyed by all."

"Each of you knows me differently, but for the same reason. Some of you wish this could all be done another way and are angry. Some of you are excited for the journey ahead. Some of you are friends, but the promise I am making is equal to all of you."

"I will forge your medallion today. It will be our bond, and my promise is to always be available to you at this place or when called upon by you while you are fulfilling your task, wherever and whenever that may be. I'm doing this with you. You are not doing this for me. We are doing this because it is right to stop the abuse of magic, which will destroy us all. This is a good cause that will help everyone. And anyone it upsets is the very one that must be stopped. Their abuse must end."

He went on: "I've lit the cauldron. I have prepared my chalice. You have your scroll, which we wrote together privately and sealed that night. There is ink awaiting your hand. Sign your scroll, light it, and stoke the fire. But first, is there anyone among us—and there is no shame in this—who would prefer that their medallion never be forged?"

She watched as each person went to the podium by the cauldron. Each signed their name on their scroll. Each tossed it into the fire. As the fire remained strong with each scroll, the silver was poured to fill the mold on the curious table. Each medallion was stamped by the Teacher using the bottom of his chalice. The Teacher was the last to roll his scrolls, each with his signature. One he placed in his robe and the other in the furnace, and the fire belched one more tuft of flame while the cauldron bubbled one last time in earnest to forge his medallion. The cauldron was poured and left in its final position while the last of the silver hit the stone. As soon as the chalice base hit the silver, the cauldron turned to dust, and the contraption holding it above the flame fell apart in pieces, scattering across the floor. The flame blew to the ceiling of the room with a rumbling clap and a huge Poof of smoke, and it was immediately put out. There wasn't even so much as a trace of smoke as it ended. The final liquid from the chalice was poured onto the molting silver, cooling it and causing the steam just as he had done to each other's medallions. On this last medallion, the chalice turned to dust in his hands like the cauldron.

He smiled at everyone as he motioned with his hands to retrieve his medallion.

The instant his hand touched the coin, everyone vanished. He remained unflappable as it occurred. He simply took it and placed it in his pocket.

The only two in the room were him and her. They didn't speak. He took the scroll out of his robe. He brought it to a table where a small flame and wax were waiting. He sat on a small chair. He poured some wax on the scroll and pressed his newly forged coin against it to seal it. He handed it to her. She nodded and left the room.

He remained seated in the chair. He sat alone in an enormous room, where no trace of anything that had just occurred was left.

The cat jumped onto his lap. He scritched her neck and said, "And now we wait, Minnie. And now we wait."

Scene 2 | ... and now we wait

The year is 450

The cat jumped onto his lap. He scritched her neck and said, "And now we wait, Minnie. And now we wait."

What he had planned to do was have some tea right after the whole ordeal. But as he headed to put the kettle on, he realized he had a bit of a mess to clean up instead, and the fire was now out. He hadn't really thought about how it would actually end, with everything falling apart and the fire blowing up and out as it did. He clearly hadn't thought it through enough to realize that there would be a mess to clean up, and he laughed at himself. In his head, he was thinking about how he really should be better about planning the things that come right after any big ordeal. There's always a mess to clean up. He knew this.

So, he got to it. He figured he would have tea that night and try making some new cakes. That would complete the first day of what he would grow to call *the great magic renewal*. It would grow to that title over time in his head. He had only officially referred to it as *the mess* so far that day, and he began picking up pieces and tossing them into the fireplace. He did take notice that his ever-burning candle remained lit through it all, so he planned to use it to restart his fire once everything was cleaned up.

He kept that candle lit on a small side table by his favorite chair. It was the only green-cloth chair (with a subtle stripe pattern) in the whole place. Everything else was leather or a solid form of white or brown cloth. But his green chair was the one he sat in the most and gazed at the flame from his candle while he pondered his next thing to keep himself busy. It burned an oil that he made himself from pressing olives. He was quite proud of the candle and loved his chair. He'd had the candle for a very long time, going all the way back to when oil was first pressed from olives for burning. That was a fantastic discovery for everyone around, and so he kept his little candle as a sort of challenge to see how long he could keep it going. He had made two but gave one away as a special gift. Burning oil wasn't the only innovation he had been witness to. He even had a hand in some of them along the way, and seeing his candle always helped him reminisce... keep things fresh in his mind, and encourage him to think of all that the future could and would bring.

Once he had finally cleaned everything up, he brought some straw to his candle to transfer the flame to his fireplace. He already had his kettle on the long hook over where the flame would eventually be, so he was back on track, he reasoned. He prepared his tea in his cup in another room he accessed behind the greenhouse without any walls. And he remained silent, pondering, for the rest of his first night alone.

Every day following the *great mess* ended with tea while he took refuge in his green chair. For the next week, he sat alone in his great home, mainly by design, to be sure he was ready for his first returning visitor. He kept himself busy each day, taking long walks during the day in the bright sunlight, which he always enjoyed, and tending to his plants almost fully for a day. He walked about his grounds in the evening, taking in the moon and stars. And then he had his cat to tend to, the goats to milk, and all the birds that would come and go to the little piles of seeds he left out. He even found he was spending extra time by the shallow stream near the edge of his grounds, where the little fish seemed to play. A solitary life for him, for a week anyway, seemed very focusing, and he loved that time alone. It wasn't his first or last time alone for an extended period of time. He had grown quite capable of keeping busy none the less.

The last task he completed quickly in the morning of what would turn out to be his final day before being able to rest again. He cleared his study. He kept one room mostly to himself. Very few had ever been in that one room of the castle. He was pretty sure no one was aware it even existed as a room in the great house. The door was somewhat concealed in the bricks, stone, and wood just past the entrance room for the whole castle. Everyone who would come and go would pass the door, but if you were unaware it existed, you wouldn't think to open anything, much less that there was a room beyond that door. There wasn't much in it to begin with, so clearing it didn't take long at all. For years, his green chair and his candles were in this room, along with a small table and chairs and some tall wooden empty shelves against the wall just before a corner to another part of the room. And by the back of the room, there was an open cabinet where a staff of some sort leaned and a small leather bag sat. But somewhere in his history with the house, he decided to move the green chair out in the open, where he spent most of his time anyway. He could see it both ways – maybe it fit in with the other furniture, and then again, maybe it didn't.

And so, on day six, as his day was coming to an end, he headed to the pantry, where he kept his cup for tea. When he returned and was getting ready to have a seat to await the kettle of heating water, he did hear a rustling out in the entrance room. It wasn't unexpected really, but had forgotten that the he saw the pulse in his candle's flame that morning. Had he remembered, he would have grabbed two cups for tea, but he didn't. So, he was caught off guard a little.

He set his cup on a nearby table and headed to the entrance room to meet his guest.

As he headed that way, the cat joined him and seemed to be walking with him. He leaned down to pet her and said, "Are you ready for the start of the great magic renewal to begin?" he said with a smile. They opened the door together and greeted Morgan, who had just disappeared with all the rest only six nights before.

"Well, that didn't take long at all, Morgan, did it, my friend?" The Teacher exclaimed. He was both truly surprised and excited, raising his arms to give Morgan a hug.

"I think when I *landed*... is that the word that I am supposed to use for what just happened?" he started. But he did engage in the hug as he entered, and his words were slightly muffled. It was pretty clear he had no choice but to hug back.

The Teacher responded quickly, wanting to get to the story he needed to hear: "I think that will be just as good a description as any other. And since you are the first to return, it's the first I've heard it referred to by any of you. So, yes... you *landed*... and...?" He finished in the tone of a question to give Morgan the go-ahead to start explaining what had all happened to him since he vanished with all the rest.

Morgan continued still with a confused tone; not quite rehearsed for this part of his story that he intended to tell: "Well, ok. Then I guess I landed on the same day as our meeting, but I – we, the two of us – were actually far from here. Is that possible? Do we just land in faraway places to do our task?" And he stopped, as if that were a question he wanted an answer to. He was genuinely confused, and by stopping, he couldn't tell if the Teacher was intending to answer him or not. So, he waited.

The Teacher settled in a bit. And then he smiled. He too genuinely cared to help Morgan feel comfortable with everything that had happened, and it just now dawned on him that perhaps he was rushing into it. He slowed his thoughts. He answered him fondly, "Yes. What has happened is that you have been given a task to retrieve something, and you will have been sent, after you all disappeared, to the place and time where that can be best done. I used the word *disappeared* because to me, who remained right here, I watched all of you vanish before my very eyes. I assumed most, if not all, others would be sent to a time that would be in the future and far from here – maybe even further away than you were sent. I expect to be waiting for quite some time to receive all the items and dispose of them properly. It appears your task had you simply carry on in the same day, but far from here. Tell me about it. We will sort it out together."

The Teacher went on, mindful not to rush things and putting Morgan at ease, saying, "But, before you do, let me grab another cup. I was just making some tea, and now I will make some for you as well. You've been traveling. Tea will do you good. I will bring some bread as well."

"Thank you…" Morgan started and then realized the Teacher was gone, so he didn't continue. He drew a deep breath and settled himself. Despite the lie he was about to tell, he had been confused the entire time he had traveled back. It felt like life just kept going… but he couldn't figure out how he was so far away from this place. And having the Teacher explain it as everyone *disappearing* and *vanishing before his very eyes* didn't help clear things up. He never felt like he disappeared or vanished. He just remembers that he was in the field. He was shaken a little, thinking about all of it, and not sure about the lie he was about to tell. He was trying to think if the lie would still make sense. But then he realized he would have to go through with it now once the Teacher came back with another cup. It crossed his mind that the Teacher knew how this had already all happened since they had written the scroll together. At that moment, he was doubting himself and his lie even more. In his head, he was using the word *shouldn't*. But somehow, another more powerful part of his mind had already convinced him that he *would* tell the story he had been rehearsing.

The Teacher came back into the room with another cup and a small loaf of bread, as well as a seasoned bowl of olive oil. Morgan thought the Teacher was close enough to hear him as he approached, so he began, "Well... as I was sharing..." he began to say, but was quickly interrupted by the Teacher again.

"Yes... do tell me about your adventures, but let me tend quickly to the tea for us first." He set the bread and oil on the small table and gestured for Morgan to enjoy them. He then headed to the fire and kettle, grabbing his cup as he walked. "On second thought... grab that plate of bread and oil and join me over here by the fire. We will chat over here where it's a bit warmer." He finished.

Morgan gathered up the plate, and as he was heading that way, he started in, "And it was six days ago when we all met here?" Morgan asked quizzically and seemed confused.

"True enough." The Teacher responded with a chuckle. "And in those six days, I have been toiling to prepare each day. I just barely finished all my work. All I have had time to do is prepare a place for the items that you all return so that I can dispose of them as we had all discussed. I'm looking forward to hearing about the first one to return. You do have it, don't you?" And as soon as he asked that question, he waved it off and continued quickly. "Wait a minute, no, no... We will hear the whole story from the beginning, and then we will know everything we need to know. Forgive me for rushing into it all. No need to rush." He said, as he scooped two scoops of the very fine tea he had crafted

14

into the pot over the fire. "Now, continue and take all the time you need."

When the Teacher started tending to the fire and kettle, just then, Morgan had a flash in his mind where the entire truth danced across his mind like a lightning strike. After that, he didn't hear much of what the Teacher was saying.

They were on a hill when, just a blink of an eye before, they were in this very room watching a fire lick the ceiling.

Morgan could read the scroll now in his mind as if it were burned into the back of his eyes: his task was to retrieve a dagger. The scroll itself had the details of the man he would meet, who he would have met once before, and all the rest of the details. All he had to do was ask for the dagger from the man, and it would be given. There would be no fight. And since all of that seemed clear enough, his confidence in his lie grew stronger. Everything on the scroll was true.

His lie would stop there, but the flash of everything whirled like thunder in his mind, and he felt his heart pound slightly harder as the images replayed in his mind. He could hear Ambrose talking about the power of the dagger. The source of the power being written in the book. How the book was being protected and would be returned to the Teacher like all the rest of the magical items by someone in that room. Ambrose speaking about the crown he was sent to retrieve. All the topics rippled across his mind.

And then he steeled himself to withhold all of this information when he recalled the bargain he and

Ambrose struck. And making *that* decision made him feel stronger and more confident than ever.

Morgan had successfully convinced himself that the plan was, indeed, in motion and that both he and Ambrose were allies. Morgan to deliver the dagger, but only to gain the trust of the Teacher so he could steal the book from someone destined to return it to the Teacher. Ambrose to deliver the crown and continue his life as before, awaiting the help of Morgan once he had the power of the book in his possession. Morgan would have the greatest power ever known and no Teacher to restrict it. Ambrose would be a king with an army at his disposal to conquer whenever he pleased. They sealed the deal, and Ambrose handed over the dagger to Morgan.

Once Morgan had the dagger and the power it possessed, he also let Ambrose know that he could just kill him if he was going to share any of these plans with the Teacher. The power of might intoxicated him at the very moment the dagger touched his hand, and he would never allow that feeling to leave him, he vowed. He wanted more. He had to have the book.

Now all he had to do was keep the Teacher in the dark. That became even simpler for him to think of as easy when he looked up at the small man putting tea in a pot with a silly grin. Staring at him, Morgan focused again on the present, just as the memory of him and Ambrose shaking hands on the deal solidified his lie.

The Teacher was sitting and waiting patiently.

Morgan drew in his breath and spoke, "I hope I don't disappoint you, Teacher. It wasn't that eventful, nor is it that long of a story. Just like you and I discussed, what we wrote on the scroll was absolutely right. When I landed, there was another man around – a man I had just met earlier that day, as you know, in this very room. I simply asked if he had a dagger since that is what I was meant to retrieve, and he showed it to me. It was like nothing I had ever seen before, and he didn't ever talk about it or show it to anyone at the meeting that I am aware of. That was the only other time I had ever met him, just like the scroll said. And he just handed it over. I don't think we exchanged that many words at all. I didn't ask much about it. I was a little confused, if I am being honest, about what you sent me to do. If this dagger was so magical, I couldn't and still can't see how or why that's the case. Other than that, it's quite unique, like no other dagger I have ever seen. I didn't feel that it was magical. If Ambrose had ever used the magic, he would be a king, a great ruler, or something like that, wouldn't he? I don't believe he was or is anything powerful... because of the dagger, that is." And he ended that bit of the story, not as a question. It was more of a statement, and so the Teacher didn't intend to answer it, and he remained intently listening.

Morgan went on as if he had that short pause rehearsed just a bit. "But... it all makes sense since he was there too. At the meeting where we all went on our tasks, he was there, and that's where I met him." Morgan paused, but continued with, "Yes... his name was Ambrose, I believe."

"Ah, very well... true enough. His name is Ambrose. Terrific! So, this is working as planned. Where did that brief encounter take place?" The Teacher asked.

"It was in the middle of a field... or, actually, I'm not exactly sure since I had never been there before. It was a flat, high hill with several large boulders where it looked like a great castle might have stood long ago or maybe was being built but never finished. We didn't stay long. That's all I remember about the place we landed. What I learned is that others I met coming here couldn't tell me the name of the place, and they didn't seem to know about it when I described it to them. Ambrose seemed to know the place well, however. He walked down the hill with me and directed me on how to get back here for the day long journey" He finished up and stood to grab the pack he left by the door.

He continued, "Excuse me for just a moment... I will go get the dagger for you. It's in my bag by the entrance."

"By all means..." the Teacher waved him on approvingly. "I am very much looking forward to seeing it." And with that, his cat followed Morgan to his bag. Morgan noticed the cat following him and leaned down to pet her. The cat dodged his touch and jumped over his foot, crossing his step to make him stumble just a bit before he had reached his bag.

The dagger was hidden in a mess of dirty cloth stuffed in the middle of a bag with various provisions. There was nothing out of the ordinary for a traveler by foot at that time in history. Perhaps some things might be curious to anyone in modern times. Among other things, he had hard bread wrapped in cloth and a leather bag for water. All in, it appeared he was well provisioned for the journey. He grabbed the dagger and headed back.

As Morgan walked back to where they were sitting by the fire, he spoke, "I really owe Ambrose a debt of gratitude. He provided well for me during my travels back to you. I was able to hide the dagger, or protect it, in the bag he gave me for my travels."

He attempted to hand the ball of cloth to the Teacher. Instead, the Teacher moved things around and moved the tea out of the way so Morgan could place it in the middle of the small table between them.

The Teacher didn't waste any time. Once Morgan set it down, he unwrapped it, somewhat carefully but not like someone handling a delicate item at all. Once it was clear of all the cloth, the Teacher handled it with the confidence of a warrior pulling his weapon for battle. And there it was. The thing that had been created as a magical gift to protect was abused to cause more harm than could be imagined. The Teacher had not seen this dagger before but seemed utterly at one with it as he handled it and looked it over. To Morgan's surprise, how he handled it and the swiftness with which he pulled it from the pile of cloth startled him. And he looked on in a little bit of fear, a little bit of surprise, and a little bit of expectation to see something magical, bright, or maybe loud happen. None of which happened.

The Teacher simply finished his inspection and placed it with authority on the table in front of him, indicating that it was now his responsibility to carry out the final disposition of all magic retrieved one by one, as promised. And then the Teacher stood.

Morgan instinctively stood as well when the Teacher said, "Well, thank you, Morgan. I will take it from here, as promised. And as for you..."

"Sir... Is it truly magic? What's its source of power?" Morgan asked with what he was sure sounded like an authentic voice.

The Teacher smiled and placed a hand on Morgan's shoulder, either to comfort, frighten, or reassure him (it wasn't clear which, but it made Morgan feel very vulnerable for some reason on top of his supreme confidence at the time).

"Morgan," he began, and as he continued, his smile faded to a very serious face. One that Morgan remembers seeing just a short week ago.

The Teacher continued, "Of course you know it is." And with that, he released Morgan's shoulder and stepped back to continue in his serious voice.

"And so, as I was saying, as for you and the completion of your task, if you recall, I can provide for you in one of two ways. You can continue your life as it is right now... choosing to serve this cause when needed for the rest of your life, or you can be free as an eagle and fly the skies free of all worries and provided for as you may need all the days of your long life. Either is magical, really. Let me know by what you do now with your medallion." He said, a little formally. And with that, he pulled a small cauldron from the side of his fire and placed it where the kettle had been for their tea.

Morgan had already made his decision, of course, but wasn't sure how it all worked or even if it would still work after lying to the Teacher. Before he spoke, he was trying to think of what else he could ask to learn where the book might be. But since he had already fooled the Teacher and returned the dagger as expected, he was certain everything was in order. The plan was in motion, so he didn't want to push it at that moment.

Life was good, and his future was set. He would just find out who was retrieving the book some other day. With genuine confidence, he said to the Teacher, "I think I will hold onto the medallion. I will serve the order with pleasure and honor for the rest of my life."

And with that, they both smiled genuinely at one another, but for very different reasons. The Teacher regarded Morgan with true pity and only a tiny touch of concern. Morgan regarded the Teacher with some trepidation, but mostly with a growing sense of superiority over him. They shook hands but did not embrace. Morgan gathered his belongings in his bag, and the Teacher stopped him as he was heading out.

"Hold on Morgan... I almost forgot." And he left the room in a hurry while just Morgan and the cat waited by the entrance for the Teacher to return.

The Teacher re-emerged with a small bag that had the eagle/pendulum insignia burned or emblazoned in some fashion on the front. "A little token of thanks. And a nice bag, I might add, to keep your medallion in as you go on in life. There is a note from me and a few things that will help you on your way."

Morgan took his medallion from his pocket. He thanked the Teacher once again and dropped the coin in the small bag. He placed the whole thing in his larger pack and walked back into the entrance of the great room to leave the way he came in.

Both the Teacher and the cat stood where they were for a few seconds after Morgan had left the building. But then they headed back into the room, seemingly in sync with one another.

Talking to the cat following close enough to almost get under his foot, "… his name was Ambrose, I believe." The Teacher scoffed as he quoted Morgan. "Why does he think he had to act like he wasn't sure of that? And I saw you try to trip him up crossing his path like that. You are a mischievous one, aren't you? Keep it up, and that's what you will be known for."

Scene 3 | Long Live the Queen

The year is 1955

It was the first coronation to be televised, and Morgan was watching from the corner of the room in the hotel lobby, where they had set up a television for everyone to watch.

The Professor remembered that day well when Morgan narrowed his focus on the royal family itself. The Professor didn't know exactly where Morgan was, but the fact that the Professor and the Queen would be seen together on television wouldn't escape Morgan. The Professor knew that Morgan would piece together the connection and try his best to finally get his hands on the book. The Professor pitied Morgan for wasting his whole life as he had.

The Professor had always been on the invite list for every coronation, by design, set in motion by the earliest king. He wasn't to be the first on the list, nor the last; he was simply to be in the mix so as not to draw undue attention. Also, he was one of the very few who had a moment to personally greet the monarch privately. Some of the few who had that privilege were politically connected. Some, for religious reasons. He was invited for an exchange of messages that had been handed down through the ages.

Everyone who had the opportunity – or privilege, as it were – to meet with the sovereign on the day of her coronation would start by offering the same greeting.

They would simply say, '*Long Live the Queen*' (or '*King*' as had been appropriate a number of times as well). The sovereign's response was always the same: a simple bow of the head. The invited person would then have a few seconds to say something of great encouragement to the King or Queen, like '*My honor to serve you...*' or '*we look forward to a blossoming relationship*' or something else of that nature, and they would move on, making way for the next.

All the monarchs had a secretary who would have prepared a short list of those they would be meeting and their significance during the ceremony. The Professor was slightly different.

No secretary knew the purpose or significance of why the Professor would be so honored. The only note about him was that he was to be invited, and that directive came from the prior monarch in their notes regarding their succession. And so, it was, without fail, for every coronation.

With this coronation, it started just as it had with all the others:

"Long live the Queen," the Professor said, just as the Queen had heard from the person just before him. She nodded but was slightly intrigued by what he might say next since that wasn't made clear to her. All she knew is that he would *prove his significance with the first words he utters in response to your bow upon meeting*.

And so, her intrigue was satisfied. Indeed, she was electrified to hear him say, "His name was Ambrose... and the scroll was written shortly after he released the dagger that was given to him by a dear friend, whose family forgave him early in his life. Your family is sustained because of forgiveness, your majesty."

Now, the Queen needed to maintain her composure once she heard him speak. She was being crowned Queen as the heir to a long line of monarchs. The history books and even her own family archives were a little less than complete in documenting how it began for them. What was lore, a fairy tale, truth, and documented history for legal purposes seemed to be constantly debated, retold, and the subject of various movies, books, and fairy tales. None the less, it was her turn.

However, the one document handed down from monarch to monarch and not shared with the public in any way was written on a scroll that didn't seem to age over time, almost as if it were magic. The private tradition with every monarch established by the first King was that they would inform the next monarch of their one task: to protect the book, or *book of words* as it had grown to be called since it had no title. Secondly, they believed that true forgiveness was the foundation of their family. They would, of course, have all the trappings of a royal life and a government in which to play a part for a great many people, but they had only one job until they were told otherwise by one man. The man standing in front of the Queen on that day.

The private knowledge of the scroll, the one invited guest without a purpose as far as the world was concerned, and the location of the book were the constants that never failed. There had been wars, untimely deaths, and government upheavals, and yet the coronations occurred. The scroll was read in private by the new monarch. The constant guest was always present. The book remained protected. This time, however, was different.

The Queen simply acknowledged him with the bow, of course, and with constant composure, raised her eyes to meet his and whispered: "I vow to protect the book of words with my very life, as every monarch before me has. You have my word... and that is my most valuable asset, as it has always been for my family." Hearing these words, as he had from each monarch before her, reassured the Professor. He always felt at ease after hearing these words because he had never really thought about what he would do if he didn't hear them. He had never made another plan. He counted on the continuity, even if it was in secret, until the renewal could actually begin.

With every King or Queen prior to this one, the Professor smiled warmly and deeply and ended the encounter by saying, '*There is no need to trade our family heirlooms on this day. Indeed, long live the Queen.*' And right then, the Queen expected to hear something along those lines, as her father had heard before her and his mother before him.

But what the Professor said instead was, "A renewal has begun. Your family's purpose will change with your son, the next King. I've not met him, of course. Perhaps I should one day, but I will leave that to you, your Majesty. Let's continue the discussion – there is much to be done. Until then, long live the Queen." And he bowed to step away, making way for the one after him to greet the her.

After her coronation, she held her son like she had never held him before. He was a young man, nearing the age of a teenager. Inside, she was happily overwhelmed with what most took to be her reaction to being crowned Queen and the emotions that certainly came with it. She knew what it truly was inside her – certainly magical – and couldn't wait for her son to one day meet the Professor face to face, as she had just done. Her son simply felt awkward being held a little too long for a young man, but he dealt with it as a Prince and next in line to the crown. The cameras were on.

The small, sealed letter was delivered along with her box on the first day she sat as Queen to review the government documents as her father had.

The letter simply started, '*An invitation to lunch...*' followed with some details. She recognized the seal and smiled since she kept her seal in a small bag emblazoned with the same insignia that had been passed down over the ages.

Scene 4 | Long Live the King

The year is 1980

The Queen stood just outside the room. She couldn't say that she knew the room well... but well enough. Her father, the King, was born in that room. She was born in that room. Each of her children had been born in that room, and now the future king's twin children were being born in the same room.

There were no special accessories because of all the royal births. In fact, it was quite plain as far as hospital rooms go. The only difference today was that this was the first time the Queen had been standing outside the door to the room instead of on the other side of it doing all the work.

When the nurse came out, she curtsied and announced that both babies were quite fine and healthy, as was their mom. The nurse giggled a bit in shy confidence with the Queen when she told her the Prince, however, was doing fine once he had the cold cloth applied to his wrist and forehead somewhere during it all. The Queen appreciated the humor but didn't let on too much just how funny the sight of him fainting must have been.

The nurse left. The Queen continued to smile. A swarm of people could be heard just outside the waiting area, where the Queen now stood alone, her heart full of joy.

The Prince came out shortly after the nurse, looking a bit overwhelmed but mostly overjoyed. He was aware the Queen knew already that both her grandchildren and his wife were fine, but he still informed her, "The twins are doing just fine. As is the Princess." He exclaimed a bit breathlessly towards the end. "This is a fine day!" he said like a father instead of a Prince or future King.

The Queen, in response, said, "You can hear them all now just outside the door there. You will make an announcement that the heirs are born?"

"Oh yes, I couldn't be happier to let the good news out." He said both immediately and excitedly. It was as if he wanted to burst through the door right then but held himself back as the Queen continued.

"No need to tell that lot outside the door about the twin's future just yet. You and they will have plenty to do before then... and I'm not going anywhere for quite some time. Congratulations, by the way, Dad." With a genuine smile, the Queen addressed her son with a new title.

"Thank you, mother. And yes, let them learn all in due time." He confirmed... and seemingly calmed himself a bit, saying it with a deep breath at the end.

Looking at her son, knowing he was fine and going to be fine after nearly fainting, she said, "Well, I shall go home now and toast the future *curators*. If I do say so myself, what a joy it will be to watch it all unfold!" She exclaimed with a small flair in her voice and a celebratory twirl of her hand, all while turning to exit.

As she spun around, he said breathlessly, turning himself, "Agreed... but right now, I shall go back in there and be what help I can be." He paused and then turned back to face the Queen, saying even more tenderly, "... and mom..." he started as she stopped to turn and hear him.

He continued, "This is truly the happiest day of my life."

She smiled wisely, as only a mother can. After a pause for the two of them to take in that moment, she said, "And that *is* magic, son." And then she resumed her exit through a side door away from where the crowd was growing louder, awaiting the news.

Scene 5 | The dagger

The year is 2004

He knew this would take some extra focus on his part, so he woke up early and prepared his coffee. But instead of sitting in his favorite green chair, he chose his study. But for comfort and insight, he brought his ever-burning candle with him. Just as he placed it on the table around the corner and sat to prepare his notes for the day, the flame pulsed. Now he had seen these pulses many times, but today's pulsing brought him to a halt as he stared at the flame. The halt wasn't brought on by fear. It was not even surprising. He was halted because of the significance, and he started to reflect on things, but he knew he didn't have time right now. One more pulse. That's all this candle will be good for, and then it will be just a cool antique like everything else in the room. He smiled, staring at the flame with that thought. He was looking forward to seeing her. He always looked forward to seeing his guests. But this guest had a very special place in his heart.

The cat suddenly jumped into his lap, startling him. Two things startled him, really. The cat jumping in his lap, combined with the thought slamming back into his thoughts about getting moving in order to be ready on time. The two things seemed to shake him out of the trance he had fallen into. So, he lovingly patted the cat and said, "So, Cookie-Jar, are you ready to meet the woman who gave me your great, great, great many times over Gramma Minnie the cat? I believe she's the one responsible for the superstition of crossing a black cat's path being bad luck," he remarked, still talking to Cookie-Jar. "Do you know how many times I saw her try to trip people up? You are just like her." He stood and let the cat jump quickly to the ground. "I've gotta go now. So you run along. Be a good cat. Stay off my chair." And with that, out the study door he went on his morning errands. The cat could come and go through a little cat door leading into the study through a window. It had been put there for Minnie a long time ago when she arrived at the castle as a gift for the Teacher. At the time, it may have actually been the first official cat door in history.

On his way home from all his errands, he was sidetracked by an open-air market. They always lured him to stop. He couldn't help himself.

Even though he didn't work full-time at a university and had no degrees, those who sold him groceries addressed him as *Professor*. It was as if those who knew him had known him as a Professor somewhere in their lives. Others he passed would nod politely but not engage him in conversation as others did. Some would ask him things as he approached. Sometimes they asked about historical things. Other times, they would inquire about his thoughts on current events. Some were happy to see him, and others simply ignored him like others they ignored as they passed by. Although he seemed to be a fixture of sorts, a *regular* shopper here, no one described him as old, if they ever described him at all – he wasn't young either, and he seemed wise enough that a title of Professor seemed fitting. He didn't walk around with a smile on his otherwise serious face, but once he engaged in conversation, a smile came quickly. He was warm that way with people but may have seemed unapproachable until it was seen how he interacted with others. In his mind, he hadn't changed in ages. People seemed to, he thought, but not in ways that mattered. He still enjoyed the smiles, cared when he saw others weep, and would offer his handkerchief or carry a bag for someone struggling. Those things seemed to be constants in his lifetime, and he was glad of that. Today he grabbed a number of unnecessary items and lugged them in a bag to his car. Unnecessary, yes, but they made sense to him and his purposes that day.

He could remember walking everywhere he went in the past. And he remembered riding a horse as well as a carriage drawn by four horses as his primary mode of transportation. He enjoyed his first motorcycle as well, but preferred cars over everything else. He loved the modern cars and the tech. And he marveled more at where he knew they would eventually evolve to. He couldn't wait for all of that. But today, the idea of using a motorcycle or a car to get around instead of a horse was something that came to him over a cup of coffee when he gave up tea for the most part. That was a relatively recent thing, giving up tea in favor of coffee. He often thought about that day and his friends from the coffee mill. That time and those friends always came to mind when he drove his newest car with all the bells and whistles. Too much time had passed since that friendship to be able to tell anyone about those days in France, so he simply thought about them fondly from time to time.

Driving home on this day was when he found himself thinking quite a bit longer about his friend than normal. He went over in his head his last visit with him, and he thought about his first visit with his old friend's great granddaughter. He had a long friendship with this family, which he cherished. They were so close that she grew up calling him Uncle. He wasn't *uncle* to anyone in his entire life, of course, so that was precious to him. So, when it came to special relationships like that, he thought it was best to hold on to them for as long as possible and wished this were more common, as a practice, in the world.

At the market, he had picked up some fresh ground coffee, bread, cheese, a couple bottles of wine, and one bottle of chocolate milk. Everything was very much like what he knew his 'niece' would have ready later that day for her guests. All he had meant to do was stop by the bank for the paperwork and meet with his lawyer. But he knew his weakness might win out today since he would be driving right by the open market. He had already made a cursory shopping list, just in case, of things he didn't need, like the wine and coffee and cheese and bread, even the chocolate milk.

He could see Michael coming from the side door entrance as he drove up the long driveway. Once he had parked, the Professor left the keys in the car as Michael opened the passenger door to grab the groceries.

"Thank you, Michael," the Professor began, "I know... none of this stuff was necessary. But you know me and open markets. Those folks selling this stuff work so hard, and it's so good. We should see if the monks can make cheese like this. They have had these goats for a long time now. I think we have enough goat milk, don't you? Will you please ask them to look up how to make goat cheese? That would be fine indeed."

Michael responded as if he wasn't paying any attention. Maybe a nod was all he did, knowing that the Professor wasn't looking at him anyway. But he did say, "Thank you, Professor. You know this is my favorite wine. Thanks again. I will have some with you later if you like."

"Great idea, Michael." The Professor said in response, but then continued, more lost in thought but still out loud, "Let's just leave the car out, shall we? I should have parked it in the front, really. Can you move it there and you can just hold onto the keys?" he said while looking back down the driveway.

Michael heard him, but he had already turned and started toward the house, and it appeared he may have missed the last bit of instruction. It didn't seem to bother the Professor at all. He knew that Michael, whether he heard him or not, would take care of it just the same. They were on the same page on just about everything, and they both enjoyed that about their relationship and roles in the world.

The Professor grabbed his unique handmade briefcase from the backseat and headed into the house once he was finished gazing down the road. The briefcase was a beautiful mix of exotic wood and leather. It wasn't perfect as most handmade things aren't, but it was well done and had lasted him ever since he had to start hauling papers from place to place.

He had found a young man at the open market when it first opened who made it for him specific to his needs. So far, it has remained exactly what he has needed. He also enjoyed the compliments it attracted from time to time. He helped him remember the fellow fondly.

Once inside, Michael headed to the kitchen to start his preparations. The Professor headed to his study to finish up his. Michael's task was simple. All he had to do was prepare the table and chairs on the driveway, move the car, and put out the new chocolate milk, wine, bread, and cheese that the Professor just purchased.

The Professor had been preparing his list of items for some time, and in this day and age, he had to enlist the help of his lawyer and deal with his bank. Nothing was new to him... just a new entanglement that he didn't like but could live with as a formality.

He knew that once she arrived, she'd need housing, money, a job, medical care, clothes, and someone to help her navigate it all... and then there'd be the baby and what that meant for them. He thought he covered everything. It was in the box. A fifteen-hundred-year jump during one walk will certainly put a person in a tailspin, he thought. When he had time, he made a mental note to really compare today's world to everything before to see just how entangled things had become. He wasn't sure what he would do with such information, but he always seemed to find someone to share his thoughts with from time to time. Maybe it would come in handy one day, but that wasn't something he could think about right now. He shook it off and carried on.

In his study, he pulled out the original quill pen that had magically remained fully functional in his room. He only touched this pen for special writing. He reasoned that using it to write a note to her on another piece of parchment would be very familiar to her. It might help.

With his whole heart focused, he wrote a note to her, explaining everything he had placed in the box he was preparing.

> *'My Dearest... I have a close friend whom I refer to as my 'niece' and she refers to as 'oncle.' She is the great-granddaughter of a dear friend, and she will meet you in France...'*

... was how he began the letter. He knew that she would read it immediately, once they were in the car, and that it would help Michael explain things to her, starting with the contraption that they both had just convinced her to get into. This was going to be a difficult day... but he remembered how lovely a day they had spent together; to her, it had only been two days. And to him, it was only yesterday in his heart. He kept all of this in mind as he focused. He had a timeline to keep today. He got to it.

Just as he was finishing up the letter, the Professor saw the flame pulse once again and knew it was the last time he would see it do that. Oddly, the room actually became a shade brighter as he blew it out, which hadn't ever been done since he lit it centuries ago. The great renewal was happening, and it added a measure of excitement inside him. But he also knew he had an immediate task at hand, and right now was no time to reminisce, which is what he loved to do while watching that flame. For some reason, no matter that he had all the time in the world, this day seemed rushed to him, and he wanted it to slow down. But the truth was that he was now rushing.

He knew she would just now be walking up the driveway, and he realized that he really should *not* have had Michael put the car out front. She would not understand what it was at all. He finished the note and sealed it quickly with his wax and medallion. Placing the note in the box, he moved with great urgency to the door, hoping to get to the car and move it before she walked up the road.

****

Although she had a good night's sleep, it had been a long week. She didn't pretend to understand everything that happened in between, but things seemed very different walking up to the castle this time. Much different than when she walked away from it a little over a week ago after everyone had vanished, and certainly different than when she was walking the grounds with the Teacher before leaving to return the dagger to Ambrose.

The grass looked different... The goats were new, and there were other things she didn't understand at all, like a fence, the likes of which she had never seen, and the type of gravel the road was made of, which looked very different from the ruts and rocks and tufts of grass she had always known. She began to doubt herself and wonder if she should be walking up to this castle at all. The Teacher tried to explain how it would feel... and a little bit about what it would mean to move to or arrive at the *time and place* to retrieve their item, but all of it escaped her now. She was scared and didn't understand why. The closer she got, the more she felt as if she might be trembling. It had been only two days since she enjoyed tea with the Teacher and walked on these very grounds. She was thinking maybe she was just overwhelmed, and then she began to dwell on each item contributing to it: helping put a meeting together where everyone disappears by magic; forgiving the man who killed her husband and giving him back the very blade he used to do it; witnessing the end of a king's life; saying goodbye to her best friend... her only friend left, forever, and she began asking *why!* to all of it, not understanding how any of it was tied together.

All she knew for sure, as she approached the castle, was that she was questioning everything, and she had never felt that before. It didn't help to see the table and chairs sitting oddly outside the front door. They too seemed wildly wrong in her mind. Something about them just seemed like nothing she had ever seen before. They were shiny white and seemed like they were cut from cloth, some sort of thick cloth she had never seen. That's all she could think of, and she wondered how they were standing there and not fluttering to the ground like a garment does in the wind. The bottles were something she had never seen before either, but she recognized the vessels. Those cups were familiar, and she almost smiled! She and the Teacher drank milk and wine from them before, and seeing them again gave her some comfort, but only some. She became more and more terrified the more she took in what was so unfamiliar to her in this very familiar place. Yet she found herself hoping above all else that the Teacher would come out and everything would be made right. This was his castle. He was the one who sent her on her task. This had to be OK, but she didn't feel it. She kept walking just the same. She was definitely trembling, and she felt it.

All her fears swirled violently and silently in her head, and her wild eyes showed the fear that so much unknown brings. Just as if he heard her screaming for him to come out and make it right, he burst through the door as if in answer to her. She was both terrified and relieved to see him with the most serious face he had. She almost fell backward and considered running away, but then he smiled and approached her with open arms, calmly and confidently. She found she was petrified and could neither run nor hug. As he embraced her, just like with Morgan and all the rest in the past, there was no escaping his hug. As for the Teacher, he was delighted that the car was nowhere to be found, and he just hoped now that an airplane wouldn't fly overhead. Michael wouldn't be able to do anything about that, and he didn't want his hug with her interrupted. She needed it, and he was happy to see that everyone had now finished their task. All but himself.

"Quite the journey you have had since we last saw each other." He began while hugging her. He didn't get a response from her, so he went on, letting the hug loosen up a bit, "True?"

"Is that true?" He repeated, allowing more space between them in the hug.

"Yes, Teacher, I am here." She replied, answering what she thought he must have asked. She couldn't quite hear him pulled into his coat as she was.

He realized his timing was off. And he thought to himself, *she couldn't have heard my question since I most likely smothered her in my coat just now.* He was always overjoyed to see those who had returned from such journeys.

So, he tried speaking again: "It's true. You are here. You have had quite the journey since last we met, yes?" And he looked her in the eyes while holding her shoulders.

"Oh yes," she started, "this morning certainly wasn't what I was expecting. In fact, this whole week has been nothing I could have expected." She paused as it all flashed through her mind in a way that made her realize how quickly time had passed in the space of just a little over a week for her. That becoming clear to her, she said, "But for you, I can't imagine. I really can't imagine." She continued to look around before settling herself on the table and chairs. They were all she could look at, and her attention was arrested there. Of everything to see on this beautiful day with a shining sun and the birds and the goats, all things she noticed in her short walk, it was the table and chair that captivated her the most. They were just so... shiny, white, and thin, and just sitting there outside. So odd.

He watched her and knew she didn't speak much about most things unless she had to. She kept a lot inside and shared what was necessary, sometimes only with her eyes. He knew that was an asset of hers. He hoped his niece could bring out all the other gifts she had. She would need them to raise a child in this day and age.

While she continued to stare at the table, she did say out-loud, "The castle seems almost the same, and Minnie seems as healthy and youthful as when last she almost tripped you up at the fire." And that memory made her smile, as it did then. That cat was a good gift for the Teacher, she thought.

Cookie-Jar was just under the table, coming towards her feet, and, indeed, was as black as Minnie was. She was almost indistinguishable from Minnie, in fact, as far as cats go.

The Professor chuckled lightly and asked her to have a seat. He might need that glass of wine right about now, he figured, and she would probably love this new chocolate milk he had for her. He was excited mostly to show that to her since he was pretty sure she had never had chocolate, much less in milk.

Her response was asked more in a clarifying tone than anything else, "Sit in one of these?" as she cautiously but confidently approached the chair Michael had prepared for them around the table.

And it dawned on the Professor that plastic was something new to her, and then, wildly in his head, he too noticed *everything* that would be new or different to her since her last visit... only two days prior to her. All he was going to do was start with Minnie, introduce Cookie-Jar, and start the learning process there with a glass of wine for him. Chocolate milk for her.

Given all the thought he had put into this day, he missed so much. It might be why he had the good sense to enlist his niece's help. Despite the problem of sitting on a thin plastic chair next to a thin plastic table holding modern bottles for wine and milk, the likes of which she had never seen before, he grew confident of his plan for her with his niece instead of him directly. He simply was not cut out for it on a daily basis, or, perhaps better said, he knew others were more suited for day-to-day care.

He headed to the table and reached for her chair to help her gain confidence in things. "Yes. My dear," he made sure to be looking into her eyes, and then he continued holding her chair for her to sit, "we have a great deal to discuss, and I want you to trust me. I've never given you a reason not to, I don't think, and today will be a very important day for both of us."

He continued just before she turned to sit in the chair he was holding, "This is something called *plastic*. It does the work of wood or metal – um, iron – when it comes to chairs and tables. And wine comes in this very interesting bottle, as does milk. As you know, these cups are good for both tea in the morning, evening and wine... or milk... for you, mid-day." He concluded his on-the-spot speech that he hadn't given any thought to prior, and began to pour the chianti into the cup for himself. And it was then that he realized he should start talking about wine instead of Cookie-Jar in order to bring her into the world in which she now found herself.

He continued as she sipped the chocolate milk from the cup. "You mentioned the castle; it *almost* seems the same. True... it's very similar to when you and I last strolled through the grounds, but so much has changed. Do you remember the wine I had with our bread that day?" he asked.

She nodded as she sipped the chocolate milk from the cup, listening intently. He continued, "Well, your milk tastes very different, doesn't it?... as does my wine." He asked her, and she continued to nod.

"Before I tell you about my wine... that is not just normal milk." He was very pleased with himself for pointing that out. She nodded and sipped even more. He went on, "It's chocolate milk. Milk and chocolate. Combined. Not the bitter stuff we had... this is... well, this is something quite extraordinary! This is new. It's new to you, and it was new to me a while ago...we will get to all that..." He really was excited, hadn't planned this part, and recognized he was stumbling a bit. He came to his senses. He was failing to explain anything to her at all that mattered. He decided to switch to talking about the wine instead. That might go better he thought.

With a tone indicating he might be starting over, he said, "My wine. You know how I am always on the hunt for a good wine. I still am, but I think I have found the very best there is."

"The grapes from which this wine comes were first made into wine about 850 years..." and he said, pausing for his next word, "*after* we had that bread, wine, and milk that day, here at the castle... which was only two days ago for you, of course. Much has changed." He smiled and sipped his wine like she was doing from her cup of chocolate milk.

She did look up at him after he shared that bit of information, "850 years. You have just been living in this house for 850 years?" Her voice trailed off, and she looked at her cup, her eyes indicated that she was trying to form another question around that, but she couldn't, and then her eyes darted to the cat, prompting her to continue, "So Minnie has been with you all that time." And Cookie-Jar just sat near the Professor's feet, licking her paw.

She looked back at him and then at the wine bottle and then at the bottle of chocolate milk and said, "Well, I really like this chocolate milk, if that helps. It might be my new favorite. I would like some more, thank you." She had finished the whole cup. The Professor didn't really notice that she had since he had only taken a sip from his cup, and he was surprised.

He stood and poured her a new cup. He topped off his cup from the wine bottle to match her full cup of milk, sat back down, and Cookie-Jar jumped into his lap.

"Let me start where I intended to start." He began, and he held the cat gently. "Allow me to introduce you to Cookie-Jar. A long descendant of Minnie, to be sure. Cats live between fifteen and twenty years in my care. I feed them well, and I leave them alone for the most part. But she is special. She is my *ninetieth* cat, and I named her after one of my favorite items in the kitchen: a cookie jar." He said, pleasantly.

She drank, taking it all in, and somehow all the numbers were too much. She didn't think they felt right, but she wasn't paying close enough attention. He carried on.

"I stopped giving them real names about the time I found this wine in France. That was a little over 620 years ago. The name I gave that cat was Grapevine. I have named my cats after things I really liked at the time they were born. But all of them have been because of the first cat you gave me – Minerva, our beloved matriarch of cats in the family. Yes. Minnie was much loved. I'm sure I thanked you for her when you gave her to me. I'm a cat person now." He concluded.

She seemed to be taking it all in rather well, he thought. He paid no mind that she was asking for more chocolate milk. He simply filled it and continued on. He was aware that people stopped listening to him from time to time, but they usually heard him, and whatever he was saying would come back to them later on when they actually needed the information.

"We enjoyed our day of rest, walking around this place in the year 450. You sat with the king of England and retrieved the dagger in the year 537, when he died after a long and beautiful life. I have been receiving items ever since, and you are now here with me for good in the year 2004, the year your baby will be born. Our work is almost complete, my dear. And I am so happy to have you here." He finished in a voice and tone that could not have been sincerer.

He had been placing pieces of bread across the table, one for each year he mentioned, separated from each other to show a timeline. It helped them both grasp the gaps in time since the *day of the mess* as he called it then, and the *day of the fire* she called it.

"Like I said, you have had quite the journey. And you are quite right – so have I." He concluded with a sigh and took his next drink from the cup.

"Do have some bread... I have a great story about this olive oil." and he caught himself before he went on about that, "But that's for another time. Enjoy it right now... I will send some with you on your journey... as well as some of that chocolate milk." And he was cut off, not rudely. She had just not been listening about the oil or bread. She just tuned back in when he had said the word *journey*, and it prompted her brain to reengage.

She asked, "So you have everything?" as she tilted her head to the side, wondering how that could be true.

"Everything but one." He started and then continued, "But I know what it is, where it is, who has it, and when it will be returned to me, so it's just a matter of time, a bit of patience, and it will all be as we had planned. Once we have that, the great renewal will be upon us. We will be able to enjoy magic as it was meant to be enjoyed and start again, and I can properly dispose of all these things I have been collecting."

She was nodding. This information meant a great deal to her, but she was now a little giddy. The journey, this new, sweet milk, all the things he needs, and the stories... Instead of her logically thinking through each of these, they were more like swirling in her mind, and she felt like maybe the sky was too as she was looking up at it. She suddenly had more energy and felt like moving now. She looked up just as she was standing up. There was a strange cloud in a line in the sky that caught her attention, and it seemed to be pulling something... or attached to something, or was it pushing something? There was something moving... She couldn't quite focus on it, and it appeared very, very high in the sky...

Her focus wasn't quite right now, and the Professor started paying a little more attention to her staring up at the sky. He looked too, and of course, it was a plane, and he felt like things were unraveling quickly. But he also knew she was probably affected by the sugar in the chocolate milk. She had never had refined sugar before, and certainly not this much in one sitting, so he decided to use that right now to get through this situation.

"The dagger... I trust you have it." He piped up with a bright voice, a little louder than necessary. But it served the purpose he intended. She snapped out of it and promptly forgot about the cloud line she didn't understand and that he wasn't prepared to explain.

He continued on now that she was looking, well, generally at him: "I will place it in my room today, and I have a gift for you."

The timing always seemed perfect with Michael. He came with the gift the Professor had referred to. It was a leather box with a simple lid that just lifted off. There were no catches, strings, or latches to hold it closed. He handed it to the Professor and then arranged everything on the table to make a bit of extra room to place the box.

As Michael tidied up, the Professor introduced him: "You've not met Michael, a very dear friend of mine. He knows all about you, and actually, today, you and he will be spending some time together on a short journey. Well, it's a long journey, but you will be traveling quite fast compared to the way you are used to traveling. And when the two of you are together, Michael will be explaining a great many wonders that will be required for you to know. I say that because I am sure you will have many questions, and he's just the man to answer them all for you."

Just then Michael extended his hand to her and said, "I'm actually quite excited to spend the time with you. The Professor has said a lot about you... and this day in particular. I hope you will be able to trust me in short order, even though you are only being asked to do so because *he* is asking you to. I am ready to go whenever you are," and then directed at the Professor, "Just say the word Professor, anytime you two are ready."

She had been listening, but wasn't sure if she had caught everything since things seemed to be moving quite quickly. She heard the word *Professor*, which distracted her since it was new and she wanted to understand. She grasped that she would be going on a journey with Michael, but thought she was staying here now since she also heard that from the Teacher earlier. She really was curious what might be in the box in front of her, and then she thought the Teacher would be going with her the way Michael just phrased it, so yes, she had questions.

The Professor knew she probably had all those questions rolling around in her head. How could she not? But he was far more concerned with her seeing the car, explaining the airplane in the sky, paved roads, lights, for that matter, and all the people and buildings she was about to experience. Modern times could very easily throw her into quite a state. He knew Michael would do an excellent job of putting her at ease with her new life. Michael had a gift for that sort of magic, and the Professor cherished it as a great asset. The renewal was indeed beginning after only 1,554 years. That might be a record the Professor thought about from time to time in preparation.

There was a pause in the discussion. Mostly because it was the Professor's turn to speak, but he was letting it all sink in with everyone. He knew she would come around quickly since this whole conversation actually interrupted her as she was about to bring out the dagger.

As if prompted, she realized that she had her hand on the dagger under her clothes, which were primarily draped cloth. A bit dusty, yet elegant in how they were wrapped or draped about her body. She was carrying the dagger, a small leather bag with some food, and another, smaller leather bag with water from the king's fountain just outside his castle. She filled it that morning when she was walking with Gwen to see the King.

She pulled the dagger from where she had been concealing it. It seemed to shimmer in the bright light of day just the same as it did in the dark of the King's chamber by candle light. It was just as stunning to her now as it was only a few hours ago. She never took a good look at it and appreciated that she could now, as the Professor wielded it about as confidently as he had with Morgan.

This was an amazing moment for her. She realized she was no longer a courier for what she understood to be the next-to-last of all the items. The great renewal was indeed beginning. She marveled at how long a week was to her when compared to the span of time the bread represented on the table. The span of time the Teacher had endured.

"Right then!" the Professor spoke up brightly, apparently very pleased. "This is a good day indeed, my dear." He set the dagger down, treating it much like his cup of wine at this point with no special attention or care. That didn't surprise Michael, but it startled her a little bit. Just a little. She was growing less and less startled by the Teacher every time she spent any time with him at all. He continued, "Michael will take you to the small house on the side there where you can get ready for your journey. I am going to take this dagger into the house and put it away as I said I would do."

The Professor was talking and moving here with some urgency, but it wasn't clear why. It still felt to her like everything was moving very quickly. Michael was standing by, ready to escort her to the guest house as instructed. But he too felt more needed to be said and that the Professor needed to slow down and take the necessary time. She wasn't moving, and so Michael didn't encourage her to.

The lack of movement prompted the Professor to turn around and see what the problem might be. He was a little confused not seeing them move, but sensed he had to say some more to make them both feel at ease. To Michael's dismay, the Professor continued with a hurried voice for no good reason: "In this box, be sure to take it when you leave for your journey, by the way." He said, as he removed the lid. "Inside is a letter. It's the top thing in there. Read it first." He was now waving it about just a little. "Nothing magical, actually," he continued. "It's all... legal stuff, really. Nowadays, it is necessary. Michael will be taking you to the home of a very close and dear friend of mine. I trust her and have trusted her entire family, just as I trust Michael and you. She calls me an *uncle*. And I call her my *niece*. She's my only one. I am certain the two of you will get along exceptionally well. It's all written in the letter..." As he finished up his little speech, he dropped the letter back into the box and replaced the lid. He gave her a wink, and without a hug or anything else, he turned to walk away with the dagger.

Michael waited. He knew that wasn't going to be the end of the conversation.

"But wait, Teacher," she said a bit louder than her voice had been up to this point. But she remained where she was. The Professor turned around, almost startled, but his mindset was of pure delight so it was no bother to him.

"Will you not be traveling with us today? Please, wait... no... that's not even my question. I thought I would be staying here with you now. Is that not the case? I don't want to be rude..." and looking at Michael, "Honestly, I'm excited about spending time with you," and then back to the Professor, "... and happy to meet your niece, but I just got here. I only just washed my face a few hours ago in front of another castle. Just a moment ago I had a rush of energy, but now I am growing exhausted. I'm not sure I can just hop on a horse for a journey," she said, and then she came to a halt as an airplane caught her eye, and the sound that goes with them followed overhead.

"And that's not something I understand... whatsoever." She said this while staring at the plane flying overhead. "That is not a bird. And it's loud," she declared, her face as calm as could be as she looked upward.

The Professor thought she might be crashing from all the sugar in the chocolate milk. Michael knew she needed to rest and to take things one at a time, and for the first time he wasn't exactly sure how the Professor was going to settle her, so he waited and looked at him to be sure the Professor knew he needed to end the conversation properly.

The Professor felt Michael looking at him but continued to look at her with delight. Delight never left his face and only increased as he walked to her, placing the dagger back on the table as he passed it.

He adjusted his chair so that when he sat, they would be across from each other and not separated by the table. He motioned for her to sit again in the chair he had prepared for her. She followed and sat in the plastic chair with the same hesitancy as she had the first time she sat in it.

Sitting across from her, he took her hands and said warmly, "Right now, you are exactly where you need to be. Later today, you will be in exactly the place you need to be, which Michael will take you to. I am only good at a few things, my dear. I choose people who are ideal for the important tasks that must be completed… tasks that I am not suited for," he explained, and she relaxed.

He continued, "Right this moment, you have so many questions, and it's right that you do. By the time you reach my Niece's house, much of what you need to know is in the box I am sending with you. Much of what you will discover and have questions about now that you are here, Michael will answer for you. And you will need a friend to live your life now, have your baby, and raise her. My niece is that friend, at least to start."

It wasn't so much his words. It was how he held her hands and focused his attention on her as if there wasn't another person in the world. That feeling brought her to a place where she was at ease, knowing things were happening as planned by the Teacher she trusted. And she was good with that. For now.

He finished up as he released her folded hands within his: "I can't be the one that gives you all the answers to all the questions you have. I can only make one promise, which I hope you will believe: the people around you will be able to answer them for you… or will be there to support you as you discover the answers."

And now he stood up, took a hold of the dagger with no special attention, and turned toward the house. He resumed the urgency he had when he first turned toward the house, intent on putting the dagger in its place.

Michael took in the answer the Professor had offered and gave an approving nod towards her when she looked over to him.

Michael motioned to the house and said, "Let me show you just a few things inside that house, and then I will leave you to prepare for the journey." He said, "I will take care of that box for you."

She stood up and followed him to the house.

She was thinking how the little house was new too as she got a little closer, but she couldn't remember what was there before. But her thoughts gave way completely to the box of things. She wanted to get to the answers and read the letter he waved around. They needed to hurry, as far as she was concerned. She had all her things under her robe, ready to get on the horse. She wasn't quite sure why they were heading into the little house at all.

As they walked, Michael had a checklist in his head of things to go over with her:

-Running water vs. a basin or stream

-A toilet that flushes vs. a basin or stream

-A bed, clothes with snap buttons, sneakers, light switches...

He had an extensive list and had practiced the route through the little house to get her acquainted.

But then, even his head started to swim a bit as he considered his list. On paper, this seemed simple enough. Reality was different. He noticed she was staring at the parked car to the side of the house. They slowed their walk to the front door.

"What is that, Michael?" But before he could answer, she was looking skyward at another plane coming from another direction.

Michael also looked up at the sky. He laughed a little, thinking how confident he was this morning about his plans.

Scene 6 | The Letter

The year is 2016

The Professor and the Queen got along swimmingly. They would meet from time to time over the long course of her tenure as Queen. Each time they met, they would dive in, seemingly picking up right where they left off the time before.

They discussed a whole host of things over the course of their long relationship. They so enjoyed time together, and with everyone simply assuming they were history buffs who enjoyed reminiscing, no one thought anything of it.

They covered the coronations – that of her son's pending coronation one day as well as those of old, going all the way back to the first. They discussed abdications, both future and past. They laughed at how various books, histories, theories, and fairy tales got some things right and others very wrong. They laughed even harder when they realized this was only for them to know... and who would believe them if they tried to fix all the stories? And how much of it mattered in light of the future? On the one hand, history is important, but on the other hand, it isn't.

They talked about the book and the dagger and the perfect timing to make the swap. They talked about the sad affair of Morgan, who had become a model employee for the Prince and Princess, none the less.

In the early years, they spoke of the Prince and his future wife and what history they would make as king and Queen... They later talked about the actual Princess when she finally appeared in the story. That gave way to talking about her future grandchildren. And then there was the actual talk about the twins when they arrived and the history they would make in the monarchy!

They also spoke of the things the Prince would need to know along the way as he grew older before meeting the Professor and how to respond to the letter he would one day receive with the Professor's private seal.

They had glorious conversations, enjoyed his cookies and cakes from time to time, and her signature tea every time they met. He'd rather have had coffee, but drinking tea with the Queen was something he looked forward to every time.

He only said it once, and he knew he wouldn't have to repeat it or remind her. It was clear the Queen understood the significance when she heard him say, "Let the Prince know that when he sees my letter with my seal arrive... he should give it some attention and allow Morgan to know of it."

He could recall the day and the conversation precisely as he said them. The Professor was thinking of those conversations fondly on the day that he pulled his pen from the desk. He always loved pulling that pen. It focused him in a way nothing else ever did. It was only pulled out for the most important of messages, and he treasured having friends that would recognize its ink and the seal that went with it.

He knew the Queen would give her son a thorough heads-up, but that only made writing the letter that much more enjoyable. Early in the letter, he wanted to simply put a few things in perspective, so both he and the Prince would be on the same page as to all the ingredients:

> *... indeed, 2016 is very special!*
> *Congratulations on 40 years of marriage!*
> *Congratulations to your children on*
> *celebrating their 36th birthdays.*
> *Congratulations on the announcement of*
> *your ascension to the throne in three*
> *short years when the Queen turns 80!...*

After a few paragraphs, he got to the meat of the letter, which the Prince had obviously anticipated after recognizing the seal.

> *...as you know, I have come into*
> *possession of an heirloom that belongs to*
> *your family. It was a gift, and I can trace*
> *the history without question to your*
> *family. I wish to meet in person to return*
> *it before your coronation.*
>
> *The Queen has also let me know that you*
> *have a valuable book that she believes*
> *belongs in my care. I am happy to make*
> *an exchange when we meet. I will leave it*
> *to you for any arrangements.*

He didn't cover much else of importance in the letter to keep it to the point. There was no value in confusing matters for anyone.

Once he finished the letter, he stared a long while at it. He knew how Morgan would react. Throughout history, he had been so predictable. However, the Professor had never met the Prince in person. He felt as if he knew him through all his visits with the Queen and his growing up in front of the television camera. But, as he reread the letter, he wondered how cool the Prince would be in letting Morgan in on the big plan – or would he blow it? He brushed aside his reservations, reasoning that if he were a shade of who the Queen was, there was no doubt he was cool enough.

****

Morgan stared at the seal. Confused. Morgan hadn't seen the Teacher's ancient seal since, oh, centuries ago, when they all sealed their scrolls. As far as he knew, this seal hadn't been used by the Teacher since.

Of course, it had been used sparingly since then, but Morgan wouldn't have known that.

So, Morgan wondered why the Prince would be receiving a letter sealed by the Teacher and written in ancient ink. He knew the Queen and the Professor were friends, but he wasn't aware of any time in history when the Prince had met him. And the Prince wouldn't recognize the ink or the seal. Something wasn't adding up for Morgan, but he didn't dwell on it. Instead he wanted to know if the letter spoke of the book.

"Your Royal Highness," Morgan addressed the Prince, bringing him the mail for the day with the sealed letter on top.

Morgan continued, "I have the daily mail for you; it just arrived, sir. I've placed the most interesting on top for you."

"Thank you, Morgan. You are the timeliest person on our entire staff. I do appreciate that. You miss nothing. You can leave it on my desk... I'm just going to refresh my tea." The Prince said.

Morgan felt the compliment gave him a little room to push the conversation forward. "Forgive me, sir. The letter I placed on top. It has a very curious seal. One I haven't seen before." Morgan had learned that the Prince didn't appreciate questions. He preferred statements, and if that statement brought up a topic the Prince wanted to discuss, he would. And likely, he would share more and speak longer than necessary. Morgan was counting on it right then.

There was a pause. It wasn't awkward. This was how it worked with these two being together for so long. Morgan would make a statement. The Prince would prepare his thoughts and decide how, when, and where he would expound on the topic, if he was going to at all.

This statement by the Prince was said as he stepped lively back to his desk with his refreshed tea to have a look at the letter on top of the pile. "Ah, yes," he started. He gathered his thoughts as he sat.

The Prince continued, "He's the old Professor from the university. Well, he's not that old." He added quickly and then mused, "I wonder just how old that man is." But then he took a sip of tea and continued, "He studies history and collects antiques, I'm told. My mother gave me an old book when she told me she planned to abdicate at her 80th. She believes it's a first edition that should be in his possession as an antique, but she's leaving that up to me. And he has a trinket of some value he has uncovered that he says belongs in our family museum. We are arranging a *swap* sometime around the time we practice the coronation, or so my mother has told me."

"But to your question about the seal," the Prince began, standing from his desk and looking at Morgan, "I'm curious about that seal as well. I've only seen that insignia one other time on a small bag the Queen has. I wonder if there is a connection." He said, brightly, as if he had just had a clever thought. He knew he had struck a chord with Morgan, even though Morgan didn't react.

"As for the letter," the Prince continued, as he started walking towards the door, "I will read it later today. I'm sure it's a thank you note of some sort letting me know what he plans to convey at my coronation. I saw that he is on the private invitation list. I've never met the man personally. He is a dear friend of the Queen, maybe one of her closest. I will ask her later."

The Prince was on his way out and making that obvious by waving to the door so Morgan could leave as well. He said as they both walked out the door, "But right now, I am meeting the twins at the foundation and am running a bit late. And the coronation is a long way off... So, there's no need to be concerned about it my friend. We will get to the bottom of it in due time."

If only the Professor could have been a fly on the wall to hear all of this. He would have concluded unequivocally that the Prince was indeed quite cool.

'... *In due time'* Morgan repeated in his head.

'*Finally*,' he said to himself as he left the room with the Prince.

Scene 7 | Ready?

The year is 2017 *(One year before Maddison meets her Grampa)*

They had been having a terrific morning together that began with each being tremendously excited to see the other after fourteen long years. The café they chose was a curious place outside of Calais. For her, the Peugeot made it in just under 11 hours. She quickly became a little too comfortable with high speeds shortly after he gave it to her. Michael taught her what it could *do* when he drove her to her new home in the south of France next door to Chantel. When she had the opportunity to take a road trip, she became excited because she would be able to *test* things to ensure the car still had *it*. She did so a few times on a few open stretches from her place to the pub in the north on this trip. For him, he would travel to France a couple times every month just to marvel at how quickly he could do it. There were so many options now, and he mixed them up from time to time. Today he drove his newest car and took the ferry. It was a last-minute decision, but the sun was out, and he thought he would grab a nice coffee and watch from the deck. He hadn't been to the curious café in years, so he was looking forward to that as well, since they seemed to add on to it every time he went there. He also enjoyed driving up to it and parking next to the horses that others had ridden over to enjoy a pint.

This location was special to him. There aren't many places on earth where an establishment has been in business doing essentially the same thing, but this was one of those places that the Teacher frequented, since... then. The very first time he came to this location, in this spot stood a one-room building with posts out front to tie horses to, and someone tended to them while riders entered to have a pint of ale and maybe some bread. It was that place where he met with more than one person to ask them to join him in renewing magic.

Since then, it has been burned down, rebuilt, replaced, and redone numerous times, always serving drinks and food and having several iterations where rooms were available for the weary traveler. And even on this visit, it still had posts for horses but also a paved parking area for cars and offered free WIFI now. Quite something. And the fact that locals still rode their horses from time to time was charming to him. He would stick with cars from now on, however.

They had already caught up on Chantel and the help she had been in the beginning, as well as the lifelong friend she was now to all three of them, halfway through their morning brunch. He asked about Maddison's schooling and general character and personality. Things he wouldn't know since he had never met her. The Teacher was delighted to learn so many wonderful things about Maddison from her mom. He was delighted to learn that she had told Maddison he was her Grampa and that Maddison would be told about the visit shortly, and they would talk about a move to England. It was as if they sat down in the morning (after comparing and talking about their cars a bit) and picked up where they left off. They both thought it was really a pleasant morning.

Maddison's mom found herself looking at him. For the first time, she was looking at him and his features. He hadn't changed much since she first arrived at his castle. She noticed that he had an interesting look about him. He had a wrinkle of wisdom across his eyes suggesting his age was in the 70s or older. But somehow, he looked much younger, and if asked, one wouldn't even guess he was in his 60s. If you met him for the first time, you'd put him in the 50s or late 40s. But learning that he was Grampa would make one wonder how that was possible. But the math could work, barely, if you tried.

"Honestly speaking," he continued, "you *have* lost touch with me for a very long time, and it was shortly after he was killed. So you won't be lying to her at all. Except for today, we haven't spoken since shortly before she was born. You are bright enough to sort out how to explain to her my invitation to you both."

"I am, and I will sort it out, as you put it. It will take some time for her to take it all in; to learn everything, and to believe everything. To understand it all... It's almost too much for me, in fact." And with that last sentence, her voice cracked a bit, as if she might weep. Certainly, she became emotional and stopped in the middle of her thoughts.

The Teacher spoke up to help her recover. He seemed to always have some of the most perfect timing when it came to knowing when to talk and when to listen. And Maddison's mom remembered that about him, hoping he would save her from crying out loud here...

"You know your daughter better than everyone. You told me you believed she was ready... to begin, and no one would know that except you. I trust you alone to know. I trust you are *righter*..." He chose the perfect word, but it sounded funny, and he hoped it would help her to smile, which she did before he continued, "...about it than even you know, because you spoke about it from your heart. I know that a mother's heart is far stronger than any thought when it comes to what is right for her child. And when it comes to what you and he agreed to, even I couldn't imagine a stronger bond being born than that when it comes to what happens now for you and her."

He became a bit more tender, and he almost reached out to touch her arm as she held back her tears while holding on to her smile, thinking of what he just reminded her of.

But he stopped short and said instead, "I wish you could see what it is I see when I look at your heart instead of what you think when you feel your doubt."

She quieted herself, and the need to weep passed. She wiped away the almost-tear from each eye. She got back to the conversation.

"She's only just turned thirteen. She'll require some time... she's still in school." She needs to complete this year where she is.

The Teacher chuckled like any father or grandfather who knows exactly what someone may have just told them but didn't need to. "Of course she will... and so will we!"

He continued, "But right now... I need time to enjoy this food. I have always loved the food here. The rooms are quaint. They raise their own beef cattle right out in the courtyard. They make a great Shepherd's pie, which is my favorite. And they leave us alone unless we yell for them. How fun is that? Are you ready for a bit more?"

She answered him with her own train of thought about the place. "This location remains magical, of course, for a great bite of food... beer and wine, and now drinks – and rooms! That's new. I am ready to order, but, I want to thank you first. I can tell you that this modern life is so much more agreeable than... before. I won't pretend to understand it all." And with that, she paused to bend her head to the side and restate what she just said, "Well, that's not true. I am completely pretending to understand it all... and that's why I am thanking you. I wouldn't have been able to do this without you. Thank you for everything you've done to ensure that I have everything I need... since we arrived. "As for Maddison and me, we're southern French girls who are doing just fine."

"My dear." He began, "You made a vow. To be clear, you made a vow to him that was far more than just marriage... a vow, I might add, that put you in grave danger, and you knew it. You agreed to fulfill that promise even though you didn't need to, even though I said you didn't need to honor that vow. Yet you fulfilled it, knowing it would put you in a place completely unknown to you one day. And not just you – your daughter. You and Maddison still have the ability to simply walk away, yet you contacted me to fulfill everything you have committed to." He took a break to drink some coffee. She took some tea.

He continued, "And now you are protecting your daughter and making sure she has the same ability to walk away if she wants to. I tell you, and I mean it. I couldn't imagine a more faithful and truer partner in all of this." He finished, having been looking at her almost sternly, directly in her eyes, for all of it. But then he looked down. During it all, he had reached out to hold her hand. He just realized that this was the first time he had held her hand so closely. He took a closer look at the ring she was wearing, something he had never done before.

He continued while looking at her ring. He continued with a series of thoughts from his heart, pausing between each thought.

"Symbols of love are powerful things. Magical really. Some of the most powerful magic I know. And yet, you thank me. All I have done... all I have ever done is teach a few good people a few good things, and I still believe they are everything. I count on that being enough, because that's all I can do. The rest is up to you and people like you."

He finished up, releasing her hand and smiling warmly at her again. "How about that for a... there is a saying, for an old dog?"

"Yes, well, that old dog will have to keep doing his old tricks. At least one more time to be sure." She smiled back, attempting to match him and conceal her remaining fear. Her mind raced as if she were holding a glass full of delicious juice... and then someone pours more into it from a foot in the air, splashing it everywhere.

She could hear everything he just said repeating in the back of her head. She knew she would be able to go over it, over and over, on her long ride back home. She was thinking about how she hadn't seen him since the day she drove away with Michael, still pregnant with Maddison. And then she began to think back to when she said goodbye to him just after everyone had vanished and he handed her the scroll. And then her brain stopped.

Time. As she was thinking about it, *time* was something she didn't understand. She knew what she had done since saying goodbye – the few days it took her to complete her task and give him the dagger. And she could comprehend the previous thirteen years spent raising Maddison. But she couldn't comprehend the time he had endured. Since that farewell, he has been alone in his castle. Her eyes went blank.

... and when the Teacher realized where her mind had wandered, he decided to interrupt and bring everything back to the present.

With a jovial grin and a rustling of his napkin, he piped up, "OK. Well, let's get this all out there as clearly as possible now that we have talked it all the way through."

"Yes." She was startled, but only in a way where her eyes needed to regain focus. A split second was all it seemed, and she was back to *now*.

She focused on him as his voice became clear to her and she heard him ask directly:

"Do you think Maddison is ready to meet me?"

She resolutely said, "Yes. I believe she is ready to meet you." Her tone. Her eyes. Her voice confirmed to him that she was still the same partner she was... then.

****

They smiled at each other, and rather abruptly, he leaned out the little doorway into the booth in which they were sitting, and he called out, "Ok! We are ready for some soup or something."

He asked, "It's rather curious, don't you think, that we have to yell for our waiter like that? It's funny how so many places have been here serving food so differently for what seems like forever from this very spot."

She was thinking that it was that way back when she worked at a place in this location. It's exactly how she and her husband met when he called out to her, except it was just a one-room pub with tables, and all they served was bread and ale. She just smiled inside at the memory, wondering how the Teacher didn't know that story.

He went on, "And by the way, I have been in contact with the Prince... Epic times ahead, really."

In the Study...

Scene 8 | Maddison

The year is 2018 *(Maddison is meeting her Grampa for the first time in his study)*

"Well, hello, Maddison." He had been standing not too far from the door when it opened. It was as if he had been tipped off that she would be coming in at just that moment and was waiting by the door when she opened it. These were the first words he had ever spoken to her in his life, and he may have spoken them a little too soon after the door was open. He was excited. She was expecting whatever her 14-year-old mind expects when told that she would be walking into a *study*. That's where her mother told her he would be – *in the study*, and she pointed her to the door. However, because what she saw upon entering did not match her imagination, or expectation, she began to focus on anything out of the ordinary. And as she did, something in her imagination made its way to her bright eyes and became part of her thoughts.

It appeared to be a castle... or a church... or something very old and very large, and it seemed strange that she would be meeting her grandfather for the first time here. She didn't think her mother was lying to her, but Maddison did feel as though the whole story she had been told was not quite adding up in her head, especially now that her imagination was mingling with what she was seeing for the first time. On the way there, her mother just said that she had only been to his *home* two other times: once just before Maddison was born, and before that, the only way her mom would describe it was by saying *a very, very long time ago* with no other comments.

This was a grandfather they had lost touch with since Maddison's dad died before she was ever born. These are the things that stuck in her memory of all the things they had talked about when it came to one day meeting him. She didn't remember being told he lived in an old church, cathedral, castle, or whatever this place was. She didn't remember being told much about anyone being rich, which he must be, she thought, as they were being driven up a very long driveway through the middle of a prairie on a very fine crushed stone roadway. On that approach to the castle, it dawned on her that they had never had a driver before, so why was that happening today? And why was her mother not talking about any of this? Every time Maddison looked over at her mom, she was just looking out the car window, and it seemed she was smiling.

So, Maddison felt at ease as well. But now all of this was piling up in her head, and her imagination was taking over. A car ride, a train ride... a hovercraft, another car ride, a train, and now this car. It never really crossed her mind why they didn't just drive like they did the last time they came to England to shop in London. But now she was thinking about it and had some questions. It was too late... they were coming up to the castle... or whatever it was.

She was remembering the moment just before they walked into the cathedral-like doors when she asked her mom, '*He isn't frightening, is he?*'

That was what was going on in her head right then. That's what he interrupted as he said *hello,* and her eyes were dancing across an array of things she couldn't immediately register all around the room. To say the least, she was highly distracted right then as she stuttered:

"h... um...hi. hello. I, I, I," but she stopped herself. She gathered her wits about her and focused on the man speaking to her; seeing his smile from a safe distance, still beaming at her, she said, "Hello, sir. I've been told I can call you Grampa, but we've only just met, and it is my pleasure, of course."

She couldn't help it. She knew she should remain looking at him for the conversation to unfold and to be polite, but she just couldn't. Her eyes jumped back to a few of the things that had initially distracted her, and she could hear that he was starting to speak.

But, then she heard herself speaking out loud instead: "What is all this stuff?" And it startled her that she had spoken out loud what she thought was only going on inside her head. She knew she had interrupted him but couldn't think of what he was saying.

Grampa chuckled and cleared his throat instead of saying whatever it was he was going to say... probably a polite welcome or compliment or something along those lines, she was thinking. "Well... I collect things," he said. He was ready to start the conversation that way; he just didn't think he was going to start it so soon. *Ok. Here we go*, he thought, and prepared to start talking about a few things he intended to cover once they were comfortable with each other, which might have been a day or two after they met, he thought, but nope.

Maddison immediately felt three things all at once and was wondering which was going to bubble up and out of her first. She was embarrassed for blurting out words meant for her own ears only. She noted that that was *rude* and she needed to apologize. She was *happy* that he wasn't at all frightening and more along the lines of the first part of her mom's curious answer, which was: *He's probably the warmest... and the most serious man you will ever meet in your life.* She felt the warmth immediately – not the serious bit yet. And third, she felt obliged to *smile*, maybe match his chuckle, since this was not how a proper introduction goes when meeting someone for the first time. It seemed a silly moment, and he was smiling, so a chuckle wouldn't hurt, she thought. But what she actually did was all three... She smiled, chuckled, and giggled a little too much, she thought, but it was a silly feeling she had, and she said warmly, matching his tone:

"I'm sorry to have just interrupted you, but all these things are... quite something." She paused, and he didn't fill the pause with any words. He remained as he was, smiling at her, and she remained determined to see everything all at once and right now. She continued, "But I don't know what any of these things are. I was distracted, and that's the truth – it just came out. Actually, I'm still a little distracted." She said this as she turned in a full circle to see everything. Throughout it all, she had progressed further into the study, while he had remained exactly where he had begun. When she came to a stop, she was not far from him at all at this point in their meeting each other.

As her twirl came to an end, he bent over a bit to be a bit closer to her height and make direct eye contact. Their eyes met for the first time, and he put out his hand to shake hers. He certainly wasn't frightening. He certainly had a warmth about him, and it was clear he was intent on shaking her hand properly. She stretched her hand out, taking his just as he straightened up.

She was thinking the whole time, *if this is as serious as he gets, that's not so bad.* "It's nice to meet you, Grampa." ... It surprised her to say that so easily since she intended to say *sir* again, but *Grampa* came out.

"It's actually my pleasure to meet you, Maddison." And he maintained eye contact for all of this while still holding her hand. She didn't look away this time, even though there was so much to see in this room and it was killing her not to keep looking. "So," she said, quite honestly, really... "Why haven't we met before today?"

That was said at the end of the handshake. His gaze lifted to the top of a bookshelf, perhaps not looking at anything specific... but Maddison's eyes followed him exactly where he was looking.

"Well... first off... It's best we hadn't met, since I would have been a terrible influence on you all these years. And the sad part is, that could be true because I've spent a lot of time collecting things over the years, as you can see." waving his hands around. "What I like to think about better is your first question: '*What is all this stuff?*' I think you asked."

He started to move slightly to another area of the room, slowly, as he spoke, "But first, some carrot cake and tea." And then he stepped back with purpose to a table further along in the room and around a corner. To her, it seemed he meant for her to follow, and she kept wondering why he looked up at the bookshelf. She looked again and saw a box, which she assumed was what he was looking at, but she wasn't sure. She made a mental note to ask about that box sometime.

"I've just made this carrot cake this morning, and it's what I intend to have for lunch. There. Do you see? Bad influence. I bet your mother would prefer we have some soup and bread, or maybe some pasta and salad." As he rolled his eyes toward the end.

It just dawned on Maddison that her mother was not in the room with them. Everything just seemed to be going so well, and although it had only been a few moments, it felt like a much longer and more comfortable conversation so far. And so, she asked, "Is my mom going to join us for carrot cake and tea? I thought she was right behind me, actually. I know she was talking to someone who showed us to your study..." and her voice trailed off just as his started up.

He answered, "When she told me that you and she were coming, I invited an old friend of hers as well. And they are, right now, in the kitchen catching up. And they are having a proper lunch of soup with salad or some such thing, so she will think you and I are having the same lunch as she is. It's perfect really. We will all meet up after lunch for desert! She is just being kind by allowing me to meet you like this in person for the first time. Your mother is a very kind woman indeed." He said. There it was. His warm smile again that seemed to make this seem like a lunch they have had time and time again. She smiled too and sat across from him. He wasn't kidding... They had cake and tea ready, and it looked really very good for lunch.

"And so... You asked, *'what is all this stuff?'* I believe." And it was clear he was ready to answer that exact question, to dive right in, but he was interrupted.

"Sorry, Grampa. I've composed myself." She started, trying very hard to sound like some sort of grownup. She continued, "I do want to know about all this stuff, but I want to compliment you first on your cake... It's delicious, and I want to know more about you first anyway." She took a bit of cake, and with her mouth full, she said, "What is this place, and why do you live here?" These questions came to her just then, as the drive up to the place popped back into her head for some reason. It seemed like a good topic.

He chuckled some more... and Maddison thought he was chuckling because she sounded very much like she hadn't composed herself at all and was talking with her mouth full, which sounded funny. He took a bit of his cake, and they just smiled at each other while they enjoyed their *lunch* for a bit. The silence seemed natural as they enjoyed the cake and he poured her some tea. He was having coffee, and when he topped off his cup, he cleared his throat.

He began, "It really is good, and I rarely compliment myself – but you said it first, and I am just agreeing. Carrot cake is one of my favorites. There isn't that much carrot in it, actually. I think it's the cake part I like the most." As he stirred some cream into his coffee, he said.

"Oh, yes," she said, reaching for her tea. "I love tea with cream. I think I prefer the cream part the most." she continued as she poured more cream into her cup of tea. "Plus, it cools it down so you can drink a little more than a sip at a time. Perfect for cake." She concluded and had a good drink from the cup.

So, he got to his answer: "This place today is a monastery. The monks run the whole thing, and I am their guest. They make the food, they blend the tea, and they tend to the goats and the grasslands all around that you drove through getting here. They make the cheese and the wine as well." He paused. "Have you had wine before? Not the kind that you buy at a store or have a taste of in church. I mean, wine that comes from a big cask right to your glass... or the kind that was put in an unmarked glass bottle several years ago and held in a cellar that you can't buy anywhere?" He became a bit more excited as he described the wine he was talking about.

And Maddison became a little confused. *'He knows I'm only fourteen, doesn't he?'* she thought. Her quizzical look must have tipped off Grampa, who carried on quickly. "Ah, you are fourteen. You wouldn't have had this sort of wine just yet." He said this as if answering her question, which she was sure she hadn't said aloud. "But we shall, all in due time, Maddison," he continued. "We shall. You see? There again, I am a bad influence."

They smiled again and had another bite of cake. She heard *monk* and *monastery* and that he was a guest... It made her ask a question out loud that she deemed *logical* before she asked it: "Why are you a guest here then... of the monks... in a monastery... that looks like a castle?" She kept adding on to her question as all the parts came to her. It was obvious she hadn't taken the time to craft an actual question. And he seemed to let her get it all out before he started to answer.

"I've lived here longer than they have, actually," he began, and then continued, "and they allowed me to stay as a guest when they came to manage everything. This entire... castle... was originally built thousands of years ago and has withstood every war and would-be conquering army since. Really, it's quite magical how it remains intact. I have called it home for my whole life, and so the monks allow me to stay. And the goat cheese is a new addition the monks started to make from the goat's milk. I really do enjoy it. In fact, I don't even like goat milk anymore and prefer the cheese instead."

Even though he didn't seem to directly answer her questions as clearly as she expected, she loved the answers because they made her think of at least ten more questions. Not only was her imagination running wild, but his answers made getting to know him more fun – and they hadn't even finished cake! He was a curious man, not a mysterious man, and she still hadn't seen this *serious man* her mom said he was. They had been smiling the whole time, it seemed. The handshake was the only serious thing that had happened since they met.

He started in again, "OK. We have to slow down on the cake... or we have to hurry up with our first piece so we can have another!" He said quietly leaning across to her with a wink. He went on, "Your mom will be joining us shortly. I told her to have a quick lunch with her old friend and then join us for dessert."

They both got busy on their cake. They both seemed to know the right answer was to hurry up and get a second piece on their plate as quickly as possible.

Maddison started up again between bites with a barrage of statements and questions. "So, this is a castle that is now a monastery for monks."

"Is this monastery a church?"

"It's curious that you have always called a church your home."

"Is your dad a priest maybe?"

"Was he a priest here? Or is he still?"

"You don't really look old enough to be a Grampa. Not really. Mom doesn't talk about my dad or his family at all... only you and really only in this past year."

During all of that, she was intent on finishing up her cake and looking at his plate as well, so they would finish at the same time. Throughout it all, he kept eating his cake, knowing she had a lot of questions but wasn't ready to stop asking them in order to hear any answers.

Once it seemed to be his turn to talk, he answered, "No, no, no, this hasn't always been a church. It actually isn't one now. It's a castle." He continued the conversation as he finished his cake at the same time she did. He shrugged his shoulders, making no big deal of the fact that it was a castle.

He continued, "And there are no religious services of any kind that you will see here at the house, which is what I call it. The monks just tend to everything that needs tending to. They meditate and ponder things, sometimes in strange places around the place or out on the grounds. I don't ask them much about how they do things. This, however, has always been a castle. It's just that no king has ever owned or lived in it. It's a private castle, or a very large home, if you will... and has been in my family forever really. Even now, I count the monks as my family. Before them, farmers owned it and tended the vineyards and beehives you saw driving in. I counted the farmers as family too. Lots of different people over the years for sure. Wonderful people and I count all of them among my family."

She let him continue. She wasn't sure if he was answering her questions or not because she had too many and couldn't remember which ones she had asked out loud.

He continued, "We shall have fresh honeycomb for lunch one day. I really am a bad influence. But you are family as well – you and your mom. And I only share fresh honeycomb with family on special occasions." He paused a little for dramatic effect and to make the joke he was about to tell a little funnier as he continued, "And, I can think of a special occasion on most any day. So, we will just pick the right day and have some."

In her head, again, Maddison had at least ten more questions, and his answers were just fun to listen to, and she found herself mostly just smiling as he went on. She heard the door open and stood, and Grampa started to stand as well.

Just as they were getting to their feet, her mom came around the corner beaming and walked slowly to Grampa. She was having a conversation with Michael that kept her attention on him, but then she noticed Maddison's grandfather. They didn't say any words. They just smiled at each other, and they embraced for a hug while mom put one arm around Maddison in that hug. Maddison felt overwhelmed right then, with tears welling up in her eyes, and she wasn't sure why. But she joined the hug, and to each, in their own way, it seemed like a reunion that was a long time coming. If anyone was looking on, it would have seemed that they were meant to be together, finally.

The younger man who entered with Maddison's mother shuffled his feet slightly, inadvertently interrupting the hug – and meant nothing by it. He frequently shuffled his feet, as if he just couldn't stand still for very long at all. He was not trying to break up the embrace, but it seemed that it did. To Maddison, he almost looked like a butler, but not quite. Something was missing. She didn't think he was a monk – but then she questioned herself about whether she knew what a monk looked like, especially in this place. Grampa broke up the hug to introduce him.

"Maddison... let me introduce Michael," he started, and then directed the next bit to Maddison's mom, "An old friend of your mother's and it looks like you two are getting along swimmingly just as before." And then generally to both of them, he said, "Michael is a trusted and true friend. He knows all about the two of you and will get you anything you need. He knows everything there is to know about this place as well... so if you have any questions, he's your man. Like I said, you are family. Let's enjoy this place as it was intended..." He paused as if everyone knew how that sentence ended, but apparently no one did. So, he raised his arms again and finished the thought: "... Joyfully!"

He motioned to the table and kept talking. "So... let's have dessert after such a fine lunch, shall we?" he announced more than asked... and caught Maddison's eye just in time to give her a quick wink. Somehow in all of that, his and her plates had a new piece of cake on them, and Michael was getting another plate all set for Maddison's mom.

Grampa was the last to sit at the table, and just as he was sitting in his chair, he resumed the conversation, "And so... let's get to it finally, shall we, Maddison? You asked, *'what is all this stuff?'* I believe."

Scene 9 | One More

The year is 2018 – *in the study*

Grampa was the last to sit at the table, and just as he was sitting in his chair, he resumed the conversation, "And so... let's get to it finally, shall we, Maddison? You asked, *'what is all this stuff?'* I believe."

"Let's start with whatever your mother has told you. What has she told you about all these things?" He started in, but Maddison's mother hadn't heard a word he said. She hadn't really even noticed that she was sitting at a table with a plate of cake. By looking at her face, she was astounded and shocked. She was looking around the room now that she wasn't as focused on her conversation with Michael as she was when she entered. She was simply unable to engage in the conversation, even though she heard them talking. She was looking around at all the things that had already shaken Maddison when she walked in for the first time. They seemed to be reacting in very much the same way except that Maddison spoke. Her mother was unable to do so.

Maddison answered him, ready to carry on, completely ignoring her mom, who was still staring at various things. "Mom hasn't..." but she stopped mid-thought once she heard Michael and her mom whispering.

Michael stepped into her mom's field of gaze, hoping to break her trance, and leaned down towards her, saying, "I clearly didn't do a good job preparing you for all this." He whispered only to her.

She whispered back to him, "No. No, you didn't. I can't believe my eyes, really. Well, I can... but I mean that this is incredible." She stammered a bit, still only to Michael. The others could see they were talking but couldn't quite make out what they were saying.

Maddison's mom lifted her voice a bit while keeping her gaze steady, seemingly inventorying each item on every shelf and in every place. "I've never been in your study, Teacher. I have never seen anything in this room, no matter..." She stopped herself from finishing that thought as another one slammed into her head just then: "So these are all the things that have been returned over the years? Over the centuries! You have them all in this study?" She finished with her voice growing a bit more confident as well as increasing in volume with each word. She stood up and walked back around the corner to where the room began, looking at each item one by one. Now she was visibly checking things off a list in her head. This was not an awestruck reaction any longer. She was making sure each item was accounted for. The Professor was glad to see her come alive. She was indeed.

The Professor and Maddison stood as well and walked with Michael to follow her. The Professor hadn't given any thought to how she might react; in fact, he hadn't really thought about the fact that she had never seen any of these things before. He knew she knew of them. He sighed as he walked. Maddison interpreted the sigh to mean he might be getting upset. Michael knew that sort of breath indicated the Professor was acting out of pure compassion like no one else could.

The Professor stepped up his pace to meet her where she was before Michael and Maddison could reach her. He stood alongside her and started in.

"Quite right, dear. You haven't seen any of this, and yes, this is everything except the very last thing. Look right here." And he walked to the dagger sitting on a shelf. "This is the one you brought me, sitting right where I put it just moments after you handed it to me out front. And here on this table is my candle, which I blew out the day you arrived. Its twin is the one from which you lit your scroll all those years ago on Gwen's table. I now keep it as a cool oil-burning candle. A relic, an antique."

"It is magnificent. This worked. Every story is here, and every secret I held is in this room. And everything he created." She exclaimed in the loudest voice he had ever heard her use. A voice Maddison had never heard before, and it scared her a little, mixed with excitement. Something was obviously happening here. Maddison had no idea what was going on, but it was happening. Maddison's mom grabbed the candle. "His work is beautiful." She concluded in a voice only loud enough for the Professor to hear.

"There is one more to collect, of course." Said the Professor, "The book." And then he continued almost under his breath, more prompted by the fact that she was holding the candle. "Um, actually, I built the candle..." but he was cut off.

She exclaimed, "The book," and with that, she looked at him to repeat it, "the book." She drew in a breath to continue on that topic but was interrupted. She set down the candle and turned to her daughter.

"Um, hold on, please," Maddison chimed in. "Can someone tell me what's happening here? My mother has told me nothing of any of this," she said, generally a bit agitated and with a voice wavering just under the surface. And then, looking at her mom, she said, "Mom, you haven't. So, this is really a weird thing going on here."

And she continued in what was quickly turning into a rant: "And Grampa, she called you *Teacher*. Michael called you *Professor*. I've never met anyone named Gwen... and Mom! What secrets are you talking about? And what do you mean when you say *Centuries*?" Her voice did crack. Emotions, perhaps... the volume, perhaps, because it was rising as well, just like her mother's voice.

Michael jumped in, still having a bite of carrot cake in his mouth, and said, "I would like to suggest that we all sit back down with our dessert." And he showed them all his cake on his plate as if to remind them visually, and then he continued, "I haven't heard anything that can't be answered. And I know that everyone is excited to be in this room right now. Um, we call this a magical moment, really – when everyone wants answers, the Professor has them, and in the end, everything is set right. I know it to be true. Every time the Professor makes cake, it works out that way." And with that, he motioned for everyone to come back around the corner to the table.

"Come..." Michael encouraged and prompted.

The Professor thought what Michael said sounded entirely reasonable and simply turned to return to his cake. Maddison still had wild eyes, and they were darting between Michael and the back of her Grampa, then over to her mother... and she kept doing it because no one else was moving. Her eyes now flared with all the questions, but no one was moving.

Michael caught her eyes the next time they landed on him, and putting her at ease, he lifted the cake plate again as if it were a lure of some sort. Maddison sighed too and let down her eyes as she started moving. Maddison's mom started walking as well, slowly, and continued her checklist as she rounded the corner, looking across the shelves.

It was a fast process for the Professor to make it back to the table. It was a much slower process for Maddison. And everyone waited patiently for her mom to make it back to the table and have a seat.

The timing seemed to work here for everyone. By the time she sat down, the Professor had finished his cake. Both Michael and Maddison were at least holding their forks as if they intended to eat, and Maddison's mom was now simply looking at the Teacher with a genuine look of admiration. He had remained steady in his commitments for literally centuries upon centuries. Magic was finally going to be renewed as it was intended, and this room held it all.

For the past fourteen years, as she raised Maddison in France, she knew this was all very real. But somehow being in the room itself brought it to life in a way she hadn't ever felt. During all that time, she bounced back and forth between missing her husband and guilt, since there were days she didn't think of him at all. She never lied to Maddison about him, but she never told her anything about him either, and that too brought on the guilt. This was a hard period of time for her since she was just doing what she knew she had to do for all of this to work. The Teacher was counting on her. Her husband counted on her. She was raising Maddison in a place and time completely foreign to her, and Maddison was counting on her. When it all seemed a bit overwhelming, she would calm herself by thinking of the friend she had in Chantel. The Teacher was brilliant for enlisting her as a friend for her and Maddison. And then she would attempt to put it in perspective. Single years piling up for her compared to centuries for the Teacher. When she thought of it that way, she couldn't comprehend it. Sometimes thinking about that helped, and sometimes it didn't. In any case, it's likely why, sitting in his presence with all the secrets right in front of her, it suddenly felt more real than it had ever felt to her in her life.

She thought it was funny that she could have all those thoughts swirl like lightning through her head in what could only be seconds. She marveled. Was it her head or her heart that made time stand still like that? She looked at the magic hourglass on one of the shelves, shaking her head with a smile when she thought of the good doctor her husband told her about. That was different... she put that story out of her head and sat.

The Professor cleared his throat and took a good sip of his wine. "One day, Maddison, we will toast you. Today, I'm raising my glass to your mom." And he did. He raised it high above his head. Strangely high, Maddison thought. Michael had obviously poured himself some wine along the way because he raised his glass high to match her Grampa. Maddison raised her chocolate milk, oddly matching the two of them. Maddison's mom crossed her arms and smiled, somewhat uneasy to be the center of attention, but she smiled just the same. How could she not? She was simply beside herself at that moment.

"To a job well done, my dear. Thank you. A toast to you for keeping your word to everyone you've ever met in your life. Not everyone can say that... and in this world, it's rare that anyone does it. Again, I say thank you." And with that, he took a good gulp of the wine in his cup.

Michael and Maddison finished with a loud "CHEERS!" as if they were old drinking buddies in a pub, and then both of them laughed. Their tone suggested they were getting along very well, and Maddison seemed just fine with just her chocolate milk for the event.

Things had been a little tense just a bit before, and now the mood was very enjoyable for everyone. As the smiles and laughter continued, the Professor just spoke as if it were part of the fun.

The Professor said, "Ok. This is terrific. I really am happy to have all of you in this room. You are the only people who have ever been in here. What do you think?" and he waved around the room from his seat.

Everyone continued to enjoy the moment, but what he said hit them hard. Maddison and her mother, in particular. It was true. As far back as Michael could remember, no one else he knew had ever entered that room. He, of course, had been coming and going for ages.

"There are no rules about it," the Professor continued. "But no one has ever needed to be in here except you." The pause he took only allowed each to have a few thoughts about what that might mean to them, and then he continued, "This room is full of marvels to me, secrets to your mom, and simply antiques as far as the world is concerned. Before that, it was rather bare. The only thing I kept in here was my rock collection." He chuckled and realized he hadn't meant to talk about that at all. But he let it slip. He went on, "Slowly, I added a few things over time. A table. A chair. At one point, I had a couple candles... and of course, I gave one of them away... to Gwen." Which is when he gestured to the one remaining candle in the room and spoke to Maddison's mom at that point. He kept going, "And I moved the chair out to the other room at one point, along with the other candle. I've since brought that back in here. And, well, eventually I had the castle built around this room. And here we are today. Magical really." And *he* even marveled at all the things in the room around them, even though it was not an overly large room.

Speaking to Maddison, "Yes, look around. I will tell you about each of them one by one." Speaking to Maddison's mom again, "But you already know how the dagger got here. More importantly, however..." and then he directed his attention back to Maddison.

"Let's answer your questions first," he started. She nodded quite eagerly and approvingly. He continued, "You know, love, that your dad died before you were born. And I know your mom hasn't spoken to you about that very much. The reason for that is because your dad and mom were just starting to fix something that was starting to go very wrong in the world. Something important had broken, and not everyone wanted it fixed. Before your father died, he told your mom the name of each person to whom a gift of magic had been given. The sad truth is that, with time, all the gifts of magic have the potential to be abused. And over time, they each were. I asked your mother to share those names with me and to keep them secret while we collect the gifts and begin anew. She was not keeping anything from you. She was honoring my request so that you could one day know about it all."

"We will get to all of it, and it will all make sense. Let me simply answer your other questions quickly to put you at ease." He continued.

"As for her calling me *Teacher*, that is simply how she has always known me. It is how I was introduced to her. As for Michael calling me *Professor*, that is how he refers to me today since I teach from time to time at the university. Its how many people know me now, rather than as a Teacher. Chantel calls me *Uncle* as you know...

and I do indeed regard myself as an uncle to her just as I regard myself as *Grampa* to you." He did drink from his wine cup at this point, and Michael was trying to gauge if this was too much, not enough, or something that just opened up new questions. Sometimes the Professor spoke too much for what people could or would listen to at any given time.

"Now for the hard part," he continued, "the secret your mom and dad had is best understood by understanding all the items in this room. Now if you want to know more about that secret, it's up to you... and we will start at the beginning, and I will share everything with you if you like. But even if you don't, ever since I asked her to keep her secret, I have been collecting these items one by one. That journey began for your mom in the year 450. The castle we are in was built around this room much earlier than that. In fact, I am quite certain it is the oldest building in the world. Keeping it up and taking care of it has been one of my many joys. And it was in this room, before there was a castle around it, that your father first called me *Teacher*."

Although he explained it with all the compassion in the world, Michael was certain that Maddison's head was going to explode or she was going to think she was in the presence of a madman. And even though Maddison's mom knew everything that was being explained to Maddison, she, too, was watching to see how Maddison would react. After all, she had done nothing to prepare her daughter to hear any of this, and they lived a normal life, thanks to friends around them in the south of France arranged for by the Teacher.

The three of them kept listening, but they also looked over at Maddison frequently to see how this little chat was going. They found themselves surprised by her response when he mentioned her dad. Maybe Grampa was not surprised, but they were.

"So... are you done collecting or not?" She said it rather bluntly, skipping completely over the mention of her dad and asking about the things in the room. She seemed unphased by the fact that this was crazy talk by any measure.

"I'm not too busy anymore." He began with a smile: "I have just one more thing to collect and have been working on it for quite some time actually. I'm pretty confident I will collect it in the next few years, give or take. There is just one potential snag that we're working on."

"You and Michael are working through it?" Maddison asked quickly, thinking she was piecing together who exactly Michael might be in all this.

"Oh, no, not Michael. He has more important things to tend to. This is my problem. As crazy as all this sounds, it's hard to believe that the last piece is falling into place now. I started working on it at the last coronation this country has seen, which was a very long time ago. And one day I will tell you all about it. I'm assuming of course that we will start with the first thing and end with the last if you want to actually hear all these stories." He finished quite satisfied that all her questions must be answered by now and that she was indeed ready to learn all about the *great renewal*. He was looking forward to taking a nap while Michael showed her around.

He took a bite of cake.

Michael took a bite of cake.

Maddison inquired, excitedly, and was irritated that he had taken a break from telling her more, "So, what was the first thing you collected?" She was beaming at her Grampa, who was now chewing on something. He looked over to her, a bit startled by her eagerness, and lamented silently that there would likely be no nap.

Maddison's mom took a big swallow of wine from a cup and grabbed the bottle to refill her glass before Michael could react.

Scene 10 | The Gifts

The year is 2018 – *in the study*

He took a bite of cake.

Michael took a bite of cake.

Maddison inquired, excitedly, and was irritated that he had taken a break from telling her more, "So, what was the first thing you collected?" She was beaming at her Grampa, who was now chewing on something. He looked over to her, a bit startled by her eagerness, and lamented silently that there would likely be no nap.

Maddison's mom took a big swallow of wine from a cup and grabbed the bottle to refill her glass before Michael could react.

"Maddison, Maddison, Maddison..." he began cheerfully as soon as he could swallow his cake, "You seem quite eager to learn. You aren't thinking I'm just a madman with an eccentric taste in antiques?" he asked.

"I'm reserving judgment." She answered. "For some reason... and I don't know why, I simply believe you. Why would you lie to me unless you *were* some sort of madman?"

"And..." she started again, but this time with a tone of pure trust that is so seldom heard unless by a child speaking to those they have learned to trust, rely on, and feel comfortable with as they start their life. "I want to know more. I feel it. I feel something in this room here with you and my mom. It's a wonderful feeling...

even though there are all these old, really cool, magical-looking things around." She paused, and no one interrupted. She wasn't done talking about what she was feeling, "I mean, there's a magic wand and a crystal ball, an old rolled up carpet that I assume flies like in Aladdin... and none of it freaks me out. I'm actually kind of excited. I don't get the centuries of collecting them and you claiming that you've all been around forever. And I want to know more about my dad. But like I said, I'm withholding judgment."

Everyone still remained silent. She felt it was an awkward silence, so she filled it. "I heard that in a movie once – withholding judgment." She concluded. And everyone felt a bit of relief because the pause *was* a little awkward, and Michael and her mom were both not sure if this was the right time or place to talk about her dad. They were hoping the Professor or Teacher would guide the conversation here away from that for the time being.

"OK. Fair enough." Grampa began. "Then, to answer your question, the first thing brought back to me officially was the dagger, brought to me by a man named Morgan." And he intended to continue on, but Maddison interrupted.

"I thought that, just a moment ago, you said my mom brought the dagger to you." And she looked at him as if something wasn't right. She was certain of what she heard him say.

"She did, love, she did. But Morgan brought it to me first. Once I had it, I made sure a good man – a dear friend of your dad's – had it for the remainder of his life to use as it was intended. And later, your mom brought it back to me. And the second thing – the official first thing I put in this very room – was a crown. It's just there in a box on the top shelf, around the corner. I put it there the day I got it. I figured I'd start at the top of the room and work my way down as things came to me."

In her head, she was smiling, and it was casting a beam of sunshine across her face. Now she knew what was in the box he looked at when she first walked in! She really did enjoy his stories. She now took a bite of cake, and her imagination ran wild, starting with a king's crown up on the shelf, and then she started adding all the other things to it that could be imagined when you were in a room like this. It was fun for her to let her mind run wild a bit. She had always enjoyed daydreaming while gazing at clouds, but this was something entirely new... or was it? She couldn't tell. Mom and Michael enjoyed their wine.

"But you know what? I think I will start somewhere else rather than with the Dagger and the Crown. They don't make much sense unless I tell you how everything came to me in the first place." He explained.

"I told you how something had gone wrong. The plain explanation, Maddison, is that this world is Magical. Truly." They exchanged a quick eye-to-eye contact where she indicated he should go on, and he felt stronger that she was indeed *ready* as he and her mom had discussed just a year ago. "Magic is all around us... but because it has been so badly abused at the hands of a very few, fewer and fewer can see it anymore. That's what happens when magic is abused and not shared as intended. Oh, the magic is all still here, but now it just isn't recognized by most, and it's been abused wildly by a few."

The Professor explained in a story-telling tone to begin, "It started with truly magical gifts. Thoughtful gifts, given to good people, meant to expand magic for everyone to enjoy. That's what everything in this room is. A personal gift." He continued with a wave of his arm around the room.

Although Michael understood magic and the *great renewal* and Maddison's mother understood it very personally, they were immediately entranced by his explanation here to Maddison. The room filled with his voice, not just because of his volume but because of something else entirely that was both sweet and awesome at the same time. It was as if the motion of his arms made them feel the way intensely moving music does from the inside out. Maddison's imagination danced across her mind in ways that a perfectly sunny day feels when it's not unbearably hot... just pleasant. Simply pleasant.

He went on, "But then those very loving and beautiful people saw something no one intended. They came to believe that not sharing magic, not showing it to others, and making it difficult for others to see meant that there was more for them."

He continued, "So, once they saw others having less, they began to see themselves having more. And they began thinking more of themselves than of others, believing *that* was how to use the gift of magic instead. Power and influence... intriguing magic, to say the least. Magic is powerful... and the temptation to abuse it is always present. That's how they passed on the meaning of magic. Broken."

Maddison felt the tempo of her Grampa's story escalate. It was a feeling that made her pay greater attention than she ever had before in her entire life. And it was a very welcome feeling that she embraced.

He continued, "They used it beyond its intention and gave away their very souls to push it to the limits of what magic can do in this world. It can both delight and destroy. It can both bring happiness and push one into madness. It brought wars and destruction to peaceful and kind people. It built kingdoms and destroyed them just as well, and all of it was done in the name of magic. The same magic used to bring fruit to an orchard and a sunset over a couple sitting on a beach, having enjoyed the day to the fullest. The same magic that speaks life, the same magic that dries tears, the same magic that lets us feel what others feel so we can best serve them as friends..."

Grampa tried to summarize his thoughts: "Now I say... which is more powerful? Blinding everyone to the gift of magic, thinking it will all be added to yourself in greater measure? Or... freely sharing it so that as many people as possible can feel it as you do."

He said it more as a statement than a question. It was obvious that the Professor could have continued, but the intensity of the room was about at its limit. The Professor felt good about having had this time to express his heart's desires and work collecting all of these things over the centuries. He thought of the modern word taught in universities, *catharsis*, and smiled, thinking this may have been the first time he had felt it and agreed with the Greeks that it was a good word. He was then brought back to his current frame of mind before an audience of three. And he focused on Maddison.

"I'm a collector of broken magic, you might say, Maddison. We began the process of restoring magic to its original intent a long time ago, when I called a meeting with some people, or better put, a band of friends and family, to that end." He said it with a finality to a story, but he continued.

"We are, right now, *renewing* magic." He said, and then continued with what appeared to be careless abandonment, "Your father built everything in this room even before he knew your mother. He was a student of mine. Magic is sort of my line of work – the real kind of magic. And all of these gifts were given to someone in order to share magic, and eventually all of these gifts were abused. He and your mother were married in secret, and she alone held the secrets of who had been trusted with these magical gifts. It was time to stop the pain that the abuse of these gifts had caused. Your father wrote down in the book of words, as I call it, just what each of these items' original purpose was, so we won't make the same mistakes again when magic is renewed." He smiled.

He switched tones not to one that sounded like he might be finishing up a great speech, "I believe the way he phrased it... *'For everything, there is a season.'* And the season of this magic has now passed. They have all been penned into tons of books as literary fantasy by authors from all over the world, and all of these things in this room will simply be antiques that can help us remember. The truth is, magic is far more fantastic than all of these... even when combined!"

Michael was certain that going so far so soon was a mistake. He quickly looked directly at the Professor, but the Professor was instead steadfastly looking at Maddison for her reaction.

Maddison looked quickly away from her Grampa's eyes into her mother's eyes, where there were tears as she looked at Maddison.

Everyone seemed highly emotional, and the room was electrified as if, for the first time, a new home was lit up with new owners, and the joy and wonder of what it means to build a home together was shining to the world through the front windows.

Maddison broke the silence, and that surprised everyone, but they snapped to attention. "OK, so normal kids in my class would think you are a madman or a really good storyteller. That's for sure." She mused mainly to calm herself a bit. But she went on looking at her mom, who was in fact silently weeping. Maybe from relief, maybe from emotions deeper than that. Perhaps because she was aware that the world was spinning in her daughter's head, as only a mother could know and a teenager would deny. Her mom couldn't stop the silent tears.

Maddison stopped herself just before she was about to be blunt with her mom about her own feelings, but then gently said, "Momma... I'm sorry you had to keep these secrets. And really... we have to keep them even longer now." She began, but then she kept speaking, bringing levity back into the room even though she was being as serious as she knew how to be. "You can't go to work and start just blurting this stuff out. I can't tell my pals at school that my Grampa is god, and I still don't really know who Michael is now that I know he helps take care of all the magic in the world in a castle that has a secret room where I had two pieces of cake and talked about drinking wine one day with my Grampa, plus now I learn my dad is as old as god and makes magical things for wizards all over the world to use... or he used to..." She continued on as it started to turn into a rant by the end, like she had done before.

Michael nodded. Inside his head, he was thinking, *Yep, he went too far.*

Mom looked at the Teacher and interrupted Maddison just as she was winding herself up. "You two ate cake for lunch? Wine? What?" and then she looked at the Teacher.

The Professor wasn't exactly sure what to make of Maddison's sarcasm/humor/anger... *what was this?* he wondered in his head. He thought the whole story he just told went great, and he looked at Michael with a questioning face. Michael broke the silence.

"Your Grampa isn't God." Michael began with a stunted voice just short of enough breath and continued, "He's a Teacher..." and realized that was barely even worth saying. He felt a little silly now. He didn't help the situation in the way that the Professor had obviously hoped or intended. But he kept talking for some reason, "Um, *Professor* actually to some people now..."

Grampa recovered and took over. He laughed out loud, knowing a whole bunch of things he had taken note of in his head while looking at Maddison and her mom. He had indeed gone too far, of course, rather dramatically now that he thought about it. Maddison was in a bit of shock having heard all of this for the first time, he knew, but he also knew she was strong and logical, and one day it would indeed all make sense, no matter what, so he wasn't too worried about her recovering quickly. Maddison's mother was indeed relieved to have this all out in the open but feared for her daughter right now as she took it all in. And so, with all that, he simply said:

"Come now... It's quite a story I just told; I realize this, but let's just take this one step at a time, shall we, Maddison? I know that, given the modern world you have grown up in, this is some crazy stuff. But, to be sure, it's all true, and you are part of this wonderful story, so have no fear." And then his voice changed slightly as he began to explain things in a way that would also protect her heart.

He continued, "You know that you and your mom have been invited to live here. I'm sure your mom and you have started to discuss that. The offer still stands. If you wish, once you move into the little house on the side, I will tell you a little more as often as I can. You said you were reserving judgment as to whether I am a madman or not, so... everything will be explained. We shall have cake when we need to. You will learn everything and have all your questions answered. Every. Single. One. And then you can do with the information as you please."

He went on since it appeared she was listening, and he could tell Michael was nodding in the affirmative as he spoke, "I will tell you about the last item I have yet to collect and every item in the room. You will learn things about your dad, your mom, and Michael, and I assure you that I will only speak the truth to you. Nothing more or less." He smiled at her as if that were a good bargain.

But then he turned to her mom before Maddison could respond. "And yes, we ate carrot cake and skipped a proper lunch like you and Michael had. I'm sorry about that. But it wasn't the first time I'd had cake for lunch, and it certainly won't be the last. And we will wait until our first Thanksgiving meal before I give her a taste of wine." And then he looked back at Maddison. Maddison's mom simply smiled and wiped her face clear of the last of her tears on her cheek with a kerchief Michael had provided at some point in all the activity.

Maddison looked at her Grampa.

"Deal." She said firmly, holding out her hand for the two of them to shake.

He shook on it.

The Renewal...

Scene 11 | Morgan

2019 | Early in the year

Michael wasn't in the best physical shape. He wasn't a big fan of exercise, but he was excited to be helping Maddison and her mother move into the small house – and not so excited to be carrying things from a truck to the small house.

But once he realized they really didn't have any heavy furniture, he found himself rather enjoying the exercise. He thought to himself that it was actually pretty exhilarating to haul very manageable boxes from the truck to the house. He had no idea that exercise could be so much fun. He also had no idea the next few days would be spent recovering from the workout.

Maddison's mom was doing just fine hauling things. She thought about how delighted Michael seemed to be to be helping with load after load. She tried to let him know that he might feel it the next day if he kept up the pace he was setting. He paid her no mind and just kept on moving.

Maddison found herself completely distracted while moving things in. She would run one way around the castle, then the other. She kept seeing things she missed along the way. Every once in a while, her mom would remind her to help move things and that there would be plenty of time to explore once they were settled. Michael chose not to say anything. *What teenager wants to be told not to explore a castle with exceptional gardens and hidden little areas?* he thought.

During the process of moving, Michael would take the opportunity each time he was by Maddison to ask some questions, trying to catch up on things.

He would ask about her plans for the summer. She would have short answers like, "Explore the castle." Or "hear more stories." Or "learn about the Crown on the top shelf." And she gave the same answer twice: "Learn all about magic, of course."

He did learn a few other things, like that she was looking forward to starting at a new school. She actually enjoyed gardening herself, so her Grampa would like that news Michael noted. He was also confused when she said she wasn't into all the crazy music, but that's all Michael heard her playing on the speaker she set up in her room in the little house. He chalked that up to her being a teenager.

And Michael learned that both she and her mom were into yoga. He inquired about it while carrying in a box containing a couple of yoga mats which he hadn't seen up close before. He thought he might give it a try some time. He was planning to get in better shape... and yoga didn't sound very hard...

Michael showed them around the grounds once they had moved all the boxes and brought supper from the castle to the little house as the sun was setting. They seemed to be settling into their little house just fine.

Michael saw that they were chatting more and more as they arranged the boxes in various places, so he decided to take his leave and give them some time alone.

They sat on the back porch. It was perfect. It was as if this little house had been built exactly for this purpose. Sitting on the sliding love seat gave way to a perfect view of the sunset across the prairie. They were both genuinely curious how the sight of *this* sunset captured their senses as it had. Back at their old home they had a field over which they could see the sunset. But on this day, in their new home, somehow the sunset felt, looked and seemed to be brand new to them. Under their breath, each used the word *magnificent*. Neither of them could remember the last time they used that word to describe anything. And using it seemed inadequate to describe the sunset they were seeing, seemingly, for the first time. They enjoyed it fully on their first night in their new home with each other.

****

The next day came. Maddison had every intention of waking up early, even before the sun rose, and heading to the castle so she would be there waiting for him in his study.

But as it turned out, she overslept a bit, and when she walked into the kitchen, she was awestruck again, just as she and her mom were the night before, sitting in the love seat on the porch and watching the sunset.

She walked to the breakfast nook, where floor-to-ceiling windows captured the sunrise perfectly over a field with picturesque trees framing it all. Her mom was already sitting on a bench, and Maddison joined her in silence. This place really was magical. Without words, as they exchanged glances and smiles, they also shared a part of their heart through their eyes. They both knew the peace they felt seeing the sunset and now the sunrise like they never had before.

Although it was later than she initially wanted, she was just fine making it to the study when she did. She saw the door was wide open, and so she bound into the secret room.

She wasted no time once she saw her Grampa. Her voice was both filled with seriousness and a fair amount of sarcasm to underscore how unbelievable this all sounded, and she said, "So where do you want to start, Grampa? I've made a list in my head of things we need to talk about."

She started rattling off her list before her Grampa even had a chance to say a word.

"My dad is a great wizard that make magical things."

"You are not god, nor are you godlike, but you are ... something that has been around since the dawn of time."

"My mom holds the greatest secrets in the world and is now at work as a baker because, well, we need the money." She stated, rolling her eyes.

Continuing without giving time for an answer from her Grampa, she said, "And Michael didn't make me clean up after breakfast this morning in your dining room. I will need another tour. I didn't get enough time to explore when we were here last time."

She went on, "And just this morning I added two things to the list."

"Who looks after all these magnificent gardens surrounding your castle... I'm guessing monks, but no one was doing it today or yesterday. And what is your cat's name? She was watching us move in all day yesterday but never came too close."

As she sat, she finished, "And I don't start school at my *new* school for another month, so... where do we begin? I like Michael, by the way. He's a nice man."

Completely unflustered, Grampa responded with the same haste in his voice, matching her excitement. He interpreted her tone as excitement anyway.

"Yes... by all means, explore all you like. You can ask Michael anything you want whenever you need to know something. And it's true. I'm not God. I am a Teacher, as Michael said. And I assure you, I am not god-like, as you've already learned, I can be a bad influence that just makes life harder for those who know me." He finished with a warm smile and a wink, which she returned.

He went on, "God is someone you know in your heart; that's the best answer I can give you. I simply have had students from time to time. And because I have a pretty good grasp of history, I teach at the university from time to time as well. At my best, I am a friend, and I have been to a great many people over time. I cherish every friendship. I have a tremendously large family of friends, you might say. And I do, indeed, consider them family."

Grampa appeared to be listening and taking note of all the topics she mentioned to cover with her... and continued, "Your dad was not a wizard... not a wizard like Harry Potter or *He who must not be named*."

Maddison leaned in playfully and whispered, "Voldemort!" and playing along, Grampa leaned in closer, he said, "Shhhhh."

But then he continued, "Brilliant author, don't you think? Fantastic books filled with fantastic magic and effects! No. He was not a wizard. But, unlike the magical items in that book, which are now literary marvels, these relics in my study are the real thing. I believe she even has one of her characters named after my very first cat. No matter... This is a real-life room with real-life things. This is not pretend or fanciful. There are no actors or scripts here. These things started it all... and were magical gifts. And then, as I mentioned the last time we were together, the people your father gave them to became, over time, sadly, full of themselves and broke things. Your dad was a great student and a terrific craftsman. Just look around. That's what he was." He paused slightly and knew she was listening.

He continued with the next thing to cover from her initial list: "I'm glad you and Michael are getting along. He really does help fill in the gaps on everything. I talk things out with him to be sure we understand things the same way. He will be able to give you insights to things I wouldn't think to tell you. I'm lucky he stays with us; he doesn't need to. He wants to, and for that I am grateful."

He wasn't finished, but he turned to have her follow her around the corner to the small table just as Cookie-Jar was coming in.

The cat's timing was perfect, and it was as if Grampa knew she was coming in. He continued, "And this is Cookie-Jar. She's a wonderful cat. She's much like the cat your mom gave me that made me the cat guy I am today. *That* cat's name was Minnie, short for Minerva." He pulled a treat from a small box on the table and gave it to the cat as he sat down, motioning for Maddison to join him at the table.

Instead, she knelt next to the cat, "hello Cookie-Jar. That's a funny name you have, little girl."

Grampa spoke up, "Yes. I have been naming my cats after things I really like for a while now. Before I moved on to carrot cake, I really enjoyed a good cookie. When this kitty came along, I was just putting a batch in the cookie jar I had in the kitchen. I think it may even still be there. It seemed a perfect name for her. She likes to hang out in the kitchen mostly and only comes in here to get a nice little treat from time to time."

He continued, "We will cover as much as we can in a month before you start classes if you like, but what was the last thing somewhere on your list? Ah, yes. Your mother's secret! Shall we start there?" he asked.

"Yes, please," she answered, quite enjoying herself in this room again. But she had been putting that list together the whole month she was away. He covered everything so fast. And he only made her think of more and more questions as he did. She was beginning to feel so comfortable just talking with him that it was as if the month went by like a flash and she and he were picking up right where they left off. She found herself actually saying in her head that it felt like magic.

When she entered, even though she was talking, she did take a quick look at the box on the top shelf near the entrance again. She was really curious about that crown, about the king to whom it belonged, and about what sort of magic she was going to learn. But that seemed to exit her mind as the present conversation got underway.

He began, "Then let me tell you about the book. The very last magical gift I have to collect. It's really quite something, this book. Every book has a title. This one really doesn't, but I have always referred to it as the *book of words*. I know, not very creative at all, is it? You might say I'm old-school. Words mean things. My students, over time, have always interpreted them in fantastic ways. And I love words because they are the building blocks of fantastic stories. And stories help shape the world around us... and when the world is shaped around us for everyone to enjoy– well, that's magic as it was intended!" He loved how all that rolled off his tongue. He noticed she wasn't all that impressed and was waiting to hear something remarkable.

He continued, "This particular book of words is something of a singular marvel. To some, it can be read but simply not understood whatsoever, and they will lose interest quickly. To others, it appears blank, as if there is nothing in it to read at all. To many... if they don't know magic from somewhere or someone, it will seem like a story written about all the different things in this room, and it won't mean much... it might be curious, but it's only fanciful at best. But it was written as a sort of love story for lack of a better description. That's how some would describe it, and I think the author leaned that way when writing it. To some, it's a full explanation of how magic works, and just like every item in this room, what can go wrong when it's abused. It's also an instruction manual, if that's what someone is looking for, that tells us what not to do so magic won't break again. Some believe it's fantastically powerful and others see no value at all. The author simply wrote it all down, and it's the last thing to be returned to me. Once I have it, I will return it to the family to whom it belongs."

"Is that the secret? My mom knows how to read this book?" she asked after a short pause when he had finished. She looked at him as if this was a bit of a letdown in the story.

"Oh heavens no. The secret your mom held is that she knew who and what families had all these magical gifts given to them by her husband – your dad." And he waved around the room at all the items.

He went on, "I'm telling you about the book because your mom was instrumental in making sure I could retrieve it. It's how she ended up here just months before you were born. She brought a dagger... I'm trading it for the book. Easy peazy." He finished up brightly.

By the look in her eyes, Maddison needed a little more than *easy peazy* so he went on a little more as a Professor than as a Grampa, "The sequence of events is this: Magic existed from the beginning. Various gifts of magic were given to good people so that they might share it and let others feel magic themselves, see it for themselves, and enjoy it as it was intended. Eventually, those good people abused the magic gifts and broke it for so many, including themselves... and really ushered in a dangerous and hard world. Over time, we stopped the abuse so the damage would not grow any larger. But the pain and sorrow and blindness to magic have indeed remained. The damage has been done, so to speak."

He continued, "Next, we will renew magic altogether, making these things nothing more than relics of the past. We will close the book on that magic, so magic, as intended, can be enjoyed by all again. Once that happens, there are no more secrets to keep. That's the good news. The bad news is that very few people today really see and understand magic anymore, so the renewal will take some time. It will take time and good people to share the magic. And then there is the man named Morgan. I mentioned him before to you, but I must tell you about him now."

And then her Grampa spoke in a tone of great concern. Maddison realized that the *seriousness* described by her mother could be this. There would be no other way to describe his face other than using the word, *serious*. That's how it looked and it was like nothing she had ever seen before, even when his story filled the room to overflowing.

He went on, "A man named Morgan pops up from time to time. He is the blindest of them all. He appears to be intent on not only keeping magic hidden, but also on blinding as many people as possible to the gift of magic as it was intended. It's worse than that, actually. He's not smart enough to actually have a plan to blind everyone and take all the power. But the damage he can cause is a by-product, and he's just unaware of the damage he could create if he had his way. You see, he thinks he wants the *book of words*. And then I suppose he thinks he can have all the magic there is all to himself and be some sort of great wizard or god or something along those lines. It doesn't work like that, but he won't take the time to learn or listen... I've given him every opportunity in the world, and he chooses to ignore them. And when he pops up, it's as if he has been lying in the grass ready to pounce and then does so rather recklessly. It's a shame, really."

It was clear to Maddison that her Grampa was sad and hurt when he told her about Morgan. His gaze was drawn to the ground... perhaps to Cookie-Jar, who had arrived and was sitting peacefully at his feet. He finished by simply saying, as he picked up the cat, "He will continue to try."

There was nothing more he needed to say about Morgan. Maddison, somehow didn't need to hear anymore and had no questions. She felt for Morgan the same way her Grampa did. It was sad to learn of him, and she took note of it.

In a much brighter tone, perhaps brought on by simply holding Cookie-Jar, Grampa announced more than asked, "You know there is a coronation coming. It's an important one. As a Professor of the university, I have been invited to attend in person, and I have a meeting and a practice of some sort to attend just prior. I will be away in London for a few days."

Maddison welcomed the change in tone and matched his bright voice, "Can I come with you?"

He answered, "No. It's a private meeting, and I can't bring a guest. This isn't a *plus-one* type thing. I will tell you all about it when I return, however. And besides... I would like to ask a favor of you while I am gone."

Surprised and excited to learn what that might be, she said, "Sure, Grampa. Whatever you need. What is it?"

He said, "I didn't forget your last question."

Not exactly sure what he meant, she replied only half kidding, "Well, I did... I have close to a zillion questions... so, answer any of them you like."

He smiled. He really did enjoy her spunkiness. She seemed to really want to go fast in everything she did, but somehow, she found a way to contain herself out of respect for him, he thought.

He said to her, "You asked who tends the gardens. *I do* is the answer. I was going to ask if you would like to take a walk with me so I can show you my greenhouse, where I start all the plants I keep in the gardens around the castle. It's more of a corner in one of the rooms of this old place... I think you will like it. It's the biggest room in the castle, and I don't think you've been in it yet. I will need someone to water my plants when I am away. Will you do that for me?"

Scene 12 | The Meeting

2019 | Midyear

It was a month before the coronation, and there was less security than the Professor expected. As he entered the coffee shop, he wasn't sure exactly what he was expecting for security, but he thought there should be something quite visible. The Queen and the Prince were already sitting at a high counter enjoying some tea, and the twins were a bit away, seated opposite each other on cushy chairs, chatting with smiles.

Just as he walked in, the twins were laughing but quickly stood when they saw him enter.

The Queen was the first to greet him verbally as she remained seated where she was: "Professor, my friend, please do join us!" she exclaimed, rather like a good friend and not like a Queen at all.

But then again, this was a *getaway*, as she referred to it in prior chats with the Professor. It was a *family get together* prior to the formal practice they were all in town for. She asked to meet at *that Ringo's coffee place the twins love so much* as the Professor remembered her words. The way she explained it to the Professor was that she wanted to *try coffee but not insult the staff at the castle who make her tea*. And she had heard good things about Ringo's from the twins.

The twins joined them at the high counter with their lattes and welcomed the Professor. The Queen took on the job of introducing each of them to the Professor by name, ending with the Prince.

The Prince smiled warmly and simply said, more in a sort of reverence but maybe a bit of awe, "It's my pleasure to meet *you*, my mother's closest friend and our family's greatest ally."

"Your Majesty," the Professor began with a slight bow of his head to the Queen.

"Your Royal Highness," the Professor said, reaching his hand out to the Prince.

And to interrupt things rather unexpectedly, one of the twins grabbed the Professor's hand, shaking it. "This is a private family meeting. There is no need for all that. We are just so honored to be part of all of this. It's really quite amazing, and we have thoroughly enjoyed setting things up all these years. We really can't wait. It will be epic to say the least."

"And besides," the Queen began saying, "we think Morgan is going to be here soon... so we wanted to save the rest of the world from witnessing whatever foolishness he has up his sleeve."

"Indeed," the Prince began, "so at any rate, I have your book, and I am guessing he will seize it. I'm trusting you can handle anything after that?"

"Well... I have to say," the Professor said, drawing everyone's attention, "I didn't expect the family welcome you've offered. Thank you for that. I'm the one who's honored, and that's the truth. But I'm curious... since you are the royal family, shouldn't there be a bit more precaution around this place for our visit? I'm not sure what I was expecting for security, but I don't seem to see any here at all."

"Nonsense," one of the twins piped up. "We came in through a back entrance attached to a flat we own. We use at a sort of office, and it's how we can get a latte without disrupting business here for the owner. It's early, and they don't open for another hour. I have a little clicker here to lock and unlock the door. That's how you got in, and I'll do the same if we see Morgan."

"We do love our lattes," her brother, the other twin, said. "We are hoping to win Granny over to the dark side. But she is still having tea, even here."

"I will try it after I've finished my cup of tea, thank you. Shall I pour a cup for you, my friend?" The Queen asked the Professor.

"Um... I think I might have a latte if that's not too much trouble." The Professor replied with a sheepish grin. He was looking at their cups and couldn't help himself. As much as he enjoyed his tea with the Queen, he couldn't resist the coffee at this moment. It's all he could smell.

"I had no idea you liked coffee..." The Queen said, but was cut off by her granddaughter.

She announced for everyone to hear, "Well... that'll all have to wait just a bit. It's time to get real, family... I see Morgan not too far off down the street coming this way."

The twins headed back to the corner where they were when the Professor came in.

The Queen took a sip from her cup of tea and remained exactly where she was.

The Prince placed the book prominently in front of himself on the high counter and appeared to be *ready*.

The Professor looked around at everyone, wondering who exactly brought the Queen her tea, the twins their coffee, and if they had somehow practiced all this. They all seemed to know what to do since Morgan was on the way.

"It really is very nice to meet you... Apparently Morgan remembered the letter I wrote you about the *swap*." The Professor said, leaning in so the Prince could hear him. He wasn't sure why he was almost whispering.

The Prince leaned in as well and said, "I almost reached out to you. Ever since then, he has grown more and more agitated. He has become a bit unstable. He's still doing his job well, but something has been brewing in that man, I fear, ever since then."

And then everything seemed to get very real, as one of the twins had said, but for a very different reason than just Morgan showing up. The Professor could see it in their eyes before he turned to see Morgan, who had just walked through the doors clicked open by one of the twins.

The Professor turned and heard the door click, locking behind Morgan, who was holding a rather large gun in one hand and his ancient medallion in the other. There was something wrong with his eyes. That's what the Professor noticed about Morgan before he really took stock in the fact that the gun was now pointing directly at him.

Once it was clear that the Professor and Morgan had each other's attention, Morgan threw the medallion directly at the Professor and surprisingly missed him even at such a short distance. It landed on the floor closer to the Queen and Prince where the Prince saw the insignia on a coin for the first time, and it surprised him a little.

With genuine concern in his voice, the Professor said to Morgan, "I already see it in your eyes, Morgan," but he didn't know how to finish that sentence. He honestly just wanted to embrace Morgan and let him know it would be OK.

But Morgan was enraged. So, this is what the Prince saw brewing in Morgan... It wasn't pleasant. He never considered Morgan to be the *rage* type, but it was clear now. Walking to the coffee shop, Morgan continuously affirmed himself that he would do whatever it took to finally have the book. Controlling that kind of power almost made him weak in the knees. But then he would take a deep breath and convince himself that he was and would be invincible, quite like the world had never seen in modern times. That kind of magic, in this day and age, would change the world on its head and make people, like the Professor and the royal family and everyone else, seem so small! If Power had a taste, he had been feasting all the way to the coffeeshop.

He barked at the Professor, "For centuries... I chased a book that you had Ambrose lie about. I thought you and your people didn't lie." And with that, he had the gun pointed directly at the Professor, not two feet away. He wasn't about to miss like he had with the medallion.

The Professor replied as if it were a question: "He didn't lie... I sent the book to be protected by someone. I sent it with Ambrose."

The Professor continued, "And every time we have met since, *you* have chosen to lie to me and to yourself about who and what you were serving. Morgan, all you ended up doing was wasting your life."

"I'm about to end your wasted life. You will be irrelevant. And everything you thought you *taught* everyone will be pointless." Morgan responded as he walked past the Professor, still pointing the gun directly at his chest. He was within reach of the box holding the book that the Prince had left prominently placed for Morgan to see.

The Professor tried one last time to appeal to Morgan, saying, "There is no need for any of this. Just stop. It's all you have to do. Stop chasing. Just stop and let me sit with you today. Just you and me."

"Seriously, Professor? That's your pitch while I stand with a gun to your chest and the book in my hands, ready to walk out of here?" Morgan replied with as incredulous a tone as he could muster.

The Professor simply continued to reason with Morgan, "Failures don't have to define you. It's true Morgan. Ambrose took a life! And the wife of the man he killed forgave him. His legacy stands before you today because of the magic she wielded. Magic, you no longer need to be blind to Morgan. I forgive you,

Morgan, just as she forgave him. That's real magic. Once you feel it, you can never be blind to it again."

It didn't seem to make a dent... but Morgan wasn't talking either. Was he listening?

The Professor continued, "All you have done is fail at stealing that which can't be stolen to be used in a way that it can't be used. All I've ever wanted for you is to live your life in abundance. It's how magic works, Morgan, for those that see it and feel it."

But the Professor had seen eyes like the ones he was looking into when he spoke to Morgan. Broken. Hurt. Lost. It's the way someone looks at the end of a long life of failing. They fail to see the magic all around them and fail to join the bigger story unfolding before them because they chase something they think is more powerful and precious. The Professor had tears that he couldn't hold back. His heart was broken for a man he loved but knew he had lost.

Oddly, Morgan noticed himself in a window reflection and thought he finally looked like the powerful man he imagined himself to be once he had the book: triumphant over people he could now consider insignificant in his life. He could feel it – he could taste the power he was gaining over the Professor.

From their distance, the twins could see the Professor's tears and the wild man in front of him wielding a gun, and they wondered if they had underestimated Morgan. Had their grandmother overestimated the Professor, his protections, and the promises he made to her over time? They wondered... and hoped... but mostly wondered. This came about much more dramatically than they had imagined it would. They felt every bit of danger one can feel. They were at a loss.

The Prince was angry. Just plain angry. He wished he had thrown the book at Morgan to get him to leave with what he came for. And then even he questioned the plan to have Morgan interfere like this. Wasn't there another way for this to happen that wasn't so dangerous? He valiantly stood in front of his mother to protect her from whatever Morgan intended to do with that gun. But he knew he had no control over this situation and regretted consenting to it in the first place.

"I've got my book. Step aside and I will leave." Said Morgan, politely to the Professor. The door clicked unlocked by one of the twins. They wanted more than anything for him to just leave or for someone to rush in and tackle the madman. Anything!

"The book will not serve you the way you think, Morgan. And besides that, it doesn't belong to you, so you can't have it." The Professor stated rather as a matter of fact.

"Fool... what do you think I have in my hands?" Morgan then began walking towards the door while still pointing the gun at the Professor.

The Professor always disliked this part of how these things went. Morgan was lost, and there was no point in being tender any longer. This man needed to see the folly of his ways.

He said in a much different tone to Morgan, "Take what you like... but you will leave the gun here. You won't be that kind of fool on the streets."

The Professor took the two steps he needed to be within arm's reach of Morgan, where the gun was. There was fear in everyone's eyes as they looked on because Morgan's expression was that the gun had fired, and he recoiled as if it had. But it hadn't. In fact, it didn't even make the noise everyone expected to hear including Morgan. The Professor simply took the gun from Morgan's hand without incident. There was no fight. There was no struggle. Just confusion for everyone. For everyone except for the Queen and the Professor. Everyone saw what had happened between the professor and Morgan. Morgan felt what he knew he felt. Yet there they all stood wondering exactly what had happened, all so quickly. The twins noticed that the queen was unshaken in every way, and the crying man they had seen before was now a man with a face that showed it felt pain, but not from a gun wound.

With genuine confusion, Morgan unintentionally asked out loud what was going through his mind: "Why didn't the trigger pull?... why didn't it shoot? I pulled the trigger three times." and his voice trailed off while he was still holding the box with the book, almost hugging it now that he had his gun-hand free. He kept walking towards the door, almost stumbling as he retreated away from the Professor and towards the door to leave.

The Professor scolded him as he set the gun down on the high counter by the Queen, "Because magic doesn't work like that. This is just a gun... Believing you can bend magic to your will because you have a gun doesn't actually change how magic really works. It's far more powerful than that, but you are blind to it. I do hope you see it one day – that you feel it."

The Professor continued from where he was, with the Queen on one side and the Prince on the other. "Morgan, I know you are going to run along now and play with whatever you think you have in that box. I do invite you, however, to come again another day when you want to talk."

Morgan just didn't grasp what was going on. But, he caught another glimpse of himself in the window and was even more impressed with the man he saw holding the box with the book and the power. Whatever confusion he had was gone. He was reassured of his own power once again once he saw his reflection. Morgan simply said, as cool as a cucumber, "No need to talk... I have the book. And your world is about to change."

And the door closed behind him.

One of the twins pushed the lock button. It clicked.

The Prince was dialing for his security on his phone and said out loud to the exiting Morgan, as he dialed, "So is yours, pal. So is yours."

The Professor pulled the dagger from his pocket rather unceremoniously and set it on the high table near the gun.

The twins slowly joined the rest of them at the high counter to have a look at the dagger.

The Prince was already connected to his security lead. "Ah, yes. Hold on just one second..." And he put the phone aside to his shoulder. He said to the twins, "Your first piece to add to the collection." pointing to the dagger. He pulled the phone back up to his ear.

"Yes... it's regarding Morgan... Come pick us up... I will tell you all about it when you get here, but you won't believe any of it, and I won't let you speak of it..." and he continued to speak to the phone as he walked away from the family. The twins grew louder as they discussed things looking at the dagger. They took a cue from their Granny to remain calm after all that, like she apparently was.

The Queen and the Professor had taken refuge in the low chairs the twins left when they came to the high counter. The twins left their lattes behind.

The Professor asked the Queen, "I'm curious. Who brought you your tea and will they bring us each a good cup of coffee?"

The Queen replied, "I'm not really sure. It was just there when I arrived. Let's just have these... I would hate for them to go to waste."

They each grabbed a cup the twins had left and took a sip of the lattes.

The Professor couldn't tell if the Queen liked the coffee or not. But he did let her know that his was still hot and delicious.

****

Morgan savored his triumphant walk to a little office he had been renting above an empty flat he was thinking of taking once he had the book. He could take the entire building... or a castle... he wasn't bound any longer.

Once he was inside, he set the box on a table in the middle of the room and stared at it. It was all really happening. He sat and recalled all the times he had gotten involved over the centuries, thinking that would be the person sent to retrieve the book. He laughed and was angry at the same time as he recalled each time it happened and he was wrong.

He wasn't exactly sure how long he had been sitting there, brooding over all his memories of failure... but he snapped to when he heard the sirens down the block. He thought nothing of it, but the presence of the box came to the forefront of his mind again.

Ah yes! The box with the book! He even said it out loud for no one to hear in his mostly empty office. He smiled joyfully and opened the box. His new life was about to begin. He pulled the wrapped book out and removed the twine holding it... but noticed a note attached as he unraveled the book.

> *This is a great first edition... But you know the real story. Please return this one to the university when you are ready to spend the day with me. ~The Teacher*

As he opened the front cover of a first edition *'Morte d'arthur'* hardbound book, he was beside himself with rage again, but this time he had a bit of grief mixed in for appearing so foolish. All the things causing him grief swirled in his head: *This wasn't the book... They've duped me, yet another lie!* The rage grew more hideous in his head! *They are even mocking me the book they chose!* He glimpsed himself in a reflection again just as he heard the door smashed in. He had a thought... but then the royal police joined him in the reflection with force and the thought left him.

Scene 13 | All the Stories

2019 | Late in the year

It took some time for things to settle down in town, the country, and even the world after the joyful abdication, or retirement, of the Queen, the coronation of the new King and Queen, and the sideline bit of news about a gun-wielding man in the presence of the royal family. And back home, the Professor reassured Maddison and her mom that all was well in the world. Morgan wasn't going to be able to harm anyone at Ringo's, not even with the gun. He was just lost. He told them that maybe one day he would be OK.

Once things seemed like they were back on a normal schedule, the Professor headed to his study. As he rounded the corner, to his surprise, he saw Maddison already there, and she had tea already prepared for them. Even though he was looking forward to a nice cup of coffee, he was fine drinking tea with her. Perhaps she had forgotten that he was mostly a coffee guy.

"Ah, Maddison!" the Professor exclaimed. "You have tea ready, I see. Thank you so much, dear. Is this our first day of *story time*?" and he headed to his wall, where he had pinned a calendar with certain days circled and a time jotted down.

Maddison smiled but was on her phone. He was confused since that wasn't actually like her. But then he remembered as he was looking at his calendar.

"It is indeed what I see," he said.

She had made her way over to stand next to him, and she turned her phone towards him to show him *her* calendar.

"Yep!" she said, delighted. "I made story time days a different color. See? Once school starts, we may have to adjust things, but I don't have the schedule yet." She concluded.

They both headed for the table where the tea was. Maddison bounded ahead of her Grampa and turned quickly before he reached the table. She put out her hands a little too dramatically to stop him. Of course, he stopped.

"I have a surprise. It's a gift... but I'm not sure you will like it." She said.

"Oh... I'm quite certain that there has never been a gift from a granddaughter that a grandfather didn't like. You are likely very safe."

She stepped aside and pointed to a new little bowl with little packets of instant coffee from Ringo's. Excitedly, she exclaimed, "You said you liked their lattes. This is the instant coffee they sell there, so you can make a latte at home like theirs any time you like! You can even make it over ice if you like. It says so on the package."

"Over ice, you say? I will have to try that. How very thoughtful, Maddison. Thank you." he said brightly. And he meant it. He had noticed the little packets in the shop as well and had made a mental note to buy some the next time he happened to be nearby.

She continued, "You and I can use the same hot water... and you can add more cream if you like... Same-same. You with coffee. Me with tea. I didn't forget you prefer coffee over tea... unless you're with the Queen," she said, bobbing her head.

And Grampa laughed out loud while sitting down to open an instant coffee packet. He said, "But there may be hope there... she did enjoy the latte at Ringo's, she finally confided after our ride back to the palace."

"That's so cool that you are buddies with the Queen. I wonder if I will be able to meet her one day." She asked more by hinting than by asking for or stating something she actually wondered about.

"Oh, I think you may... but let's not get ahead of ourselves. It's story day number one for us. Where shall we begin?"

It was really happening. It was an official story day, and Maddison hadn't really thought about where to start with the first story or even how to go about putting them in any order. She stood up and started walking slowly around the room. Grampa watched her for a bit and then stood to join her. They both seemed to enjoy the silence. She liked the imagination going on inside her head. He tried to follow her gaze, just to see what was going on in her eyes as she looked at these things.

The Professor was thinking of the various stories he would be telling her as she touched certain things or gazed at something interesting. He knew where she would land if she was intending to answer him. He was ready. He was certain she was ready too.

****

Morgan was in custody and allowed to watch TV along with all the other prisoners. He was surprised so little was said about the incident at Ringo's, but it made sense that they wouldn't let *that* story out with too many details.

He watched the news, the coronation, and the televised visit of the Teacher bowing to the King like he had seen him do with the Queen when she was so young. It was as if the royal family were the only faces on the screen whenever he walked by the TV in the shared prisoner room. It wasn't that he hated the Professor or the Prince, now king. Or even the Queen, now Queen Mother. He just wanted so much more, and he saw them as the ones stopping him from having it. He was a patient man, of course, and even persistent. He could wait this out and get his hands on the real book another time. Time. He had been enduring time since before they kept proper track of it. But for the time being, there was so much he had to just *not* say or talk about, or he'd end up in the psych ward, he mused.

The tattered old book that belonged in a museum was secure in the cardboard box locked away with his watch, keys, wallet, belt, pen, and shoes. They would be reunited one day, and he could decide then if he wanted to return the book to the Professor.

****

Maddison's mom didn't interrupt and did her best to help protect *story time* for Maddison and the Teacher. She helped adjust things with both Maddison and the Teacher as the school schedule required and as other things popped up.

Ever since she moved in, Maddison's mom made it somewhat of a top priority to catalog every item in the room, along with the name of the person to whom it was originally given and where on a timeline the gifts were given. She was certain every single item told to her by her late husband was accounted for, and she even had an appendix of other items that she didn't know about but were still in his collection. She thought it curious that extra items would be in the room, but she figured she would be able to learn about them from the Professor in due time.

Early in the summer, she walked around the castle and enjoyed the various gardens. The Teacher and Maddison would, most times, leave the study for story time and grab snacks while in other parts of the castle. She particularly liked it when, on her walks, she could see in the windows the animated stories he was telling. Sometimes they even brought the gift they were talking about with them. Maddison always seemed to be paying attention. The Professor seemed as energetic as ever when telling the stories. Sometimes they were laughing. Sometimes it appeared that one or both might be crying. She knew it was OK either way.

She kept track of where they were through the process and joined them from time to time if there was something particular she wanted to know. For sure, she intended to join them for the full story around the items about which she knew nothing.

****

Michael had his own yoga mat, and it seemed to everyone that he was rather enjoying a stretch of time with nothing dramatic happening in the life of the Professor. He had an app on his iPad and didn't let people see him doing his yoga. He was, in fact, slimming down and looking a bit more fit. Michael would come to call this one of the best summers he could remember.

****

The Queen Mother and the Professor had their next visit scheduled, but she was coming to his castle the next time, and that was a first. She wanted a tour – of everything. And the Professor thought that would be extremely fun. He was already studying recipes for the next cake he planned to master and would have both coffee and tea at the ready, not sure which way she would go. The date was set, and it would happen before he had to clear his study. That would make that part of the tour even more fun, he thought.

Scene 14 | The Curators

2020 | Early in the year

As soon as the Prince was crowned King and both he and his wife were officially acting in the capacity of King and Queen, the spotlight shifted to the twins, their families, and their eventual succession to the throne. But they didn't care. When something epic is about to happen, priorities shift. The King dodged the issue altogether, and they focused their work on the foundation. Once they had the dagger given to them at Ringo's, they could finally get to work designing the focal point of the collection around the four items and laying out the legal next steps.

When the story broke... it obviously grabbed the attention of most. But it was the second time the news aired, repeating what had been reported when it broke, that broke viewership records – in every country that measured it.

Of course, the Queen abdicated the throne on her 80th birthday to simply retire. That was big news.

But his abdication only a couple years later! Unexpected on the world stage, much less in his own country. And to have the Prime Minister announce the legal affairs of such an arrangement as "in order" was the most sensational news in the world, and everyone was hearing of it at the same time.

Headlines all over the world read something along the lines of: **The monarchy will no longer act as**

the head of any state, and instead, the royal family will be the government-approved official curators of British history, funded fully by the royal family.

They were in business – officially as 'The Crown of Great Britain', or just 'The Crown' for short, responsible for maintaining all historical artifacts and antiquities. The Royal Family Foundation is where all assets had been transferred. They became employees of their own family fortune and fully devoted to the people. They were serving in much the same capacity they had served as the Royal Family, but with a renewed focus and new purpose.

The King and the twins wrote the speech the King would deliver at his press conference abdicating as King. When the cameras were rolling and almost the entire world was watching, he spoke as if there was nothing more pleasant in the world for him to be announcing.

"'The Crown' will continue to serve all of you even as I step down as King and name my children the Curators for all historical items, properties, objects of tremendous importance, and pieces of history sitting in our various museums today held within the Royal Family Foundation. These items really belong to all of us, not just my family. *The Crown* stands for everyone, always has, and we will diligently continue as stewards for all of us. I know there are mixed feelings within Great Britain for such an announcement, but I assure you that in due time, it will become clear that this is the very best decision to be embraced by my family, this government, the people of Great Britain, and indeed, the world."

He continued, "As with any corporation, there is a Chief Executive. My wife, your former Queen and I, your former King, will serve as Co-CEO's, and we will maintain the titles of King and Queen within its four walls simply for continuity in namesake. Two curators will report directly to us, and the family will shortly invite you to a grand opening of 'The Crown', our first museum with a substantial NEW collection and their stories that the modern world has never seen or heard of quite like this."

To conclude his speech, his wife, the Queen, the Prince and Princess twins joined him at the podium. "Today, the Prince and Princess also relinquish their titles, as does everyone in the Royal Family, since we are all now fully employed serving you at *The Crown*."

Because of the nature and political impact of such a transformational announcement, the entire press conference was planned for in private and held secretly at 10 Downing Street with only a handful of reporters, who were then invited to a luncheon to discuss the announcement in detail with the Prime Minister.

****

They were all gathered in the kitchen where the only TV in the whole castle existed.

"Wow," they each said in a hushed voice roughly at the same time. The Professor even said it. But Michael,

Maddison and her mom looked at him in surprise. This was the first time that Michael was actually at a loss for words, since he and the Professor never spoke of this at all. He wouldn't have forgotten talking about this.

Maddison wasn't at a loss for words. Looking at her Grampa, she said, rather loudly given how close they were, "You didn't know about this? The Queen was just here, like a month ago. She didn't tell you? This is big... and I..."

But she was interrupted by her mom touching her shoulder as if to focus her attention since it was clear the Teacher was trying to talk.

The Grampa in him had him smiling at her reaction to all of it. He spoke lightly: "Yes, I knew... but I said *Wow* because I thought he delivered that speech rather well. They sent me a copy a little while ago... it was originally much longer, but I like this shorter version much better. It's big news, Yes?"

And he continued, "Plus... now that they have announced it, I have something to announce as well."

"They will be here later today!" He exclaimed with a bright smile, and no one knew what he was talking about. They stared at him blankly, awaiting more information.

He continued, genuinely surprised they weren't catching on. "I have donated all of these items to *The Crown* – that's the new collection the world has never seen. He just mentioned it – you heard him! This is epic! I've recorded all the stories just as I have told them to you, Maddison, in a sort of digital story. They say it will be called an *Audible*. They're reading it aloud for everyone to listen to on our phones... or whatever. Something like that. It's all quite something. They will be putting everything on display, everything here, plus everything they already have, all of it! Very exciting indeed!"

By this time, the excitement he was feeling had him end his little speech with his arms raised up and a giant smile on his face. He lowered his arms and recovered himself as they all continued to just stare at him. He said in a conversational sort of way, "We will, of course, make sure they can't be used any longer... *Turn the magic off*, so to speak."

That struck an immediate chord with Maddison who spoke up quite abruptly, "Wait... you are saying all of these are still magic?... still able to do all the things you told me people did with these things?... seriously? What... just sitting in your study... for all this time... ready to do... magical stuff?" She was almost out of breath by the end because she wasn't breathing properly, and still speaking a bit too loud for how close everyone was to each other.

Grampa replied with a surprised look as if he wasn't sure she was kidding or didn't understand something, "Well, yes, they are no longer doing those things, but... I guess, technically, yes. They are what they are and have always been... It's just that they're not..."

But before he could go back to the beginning to clear things up, he was interrupted by Maddison again, quite excited now. "I want to ride the flying carpet around the castle!... And make just one gold coin! ... and the wand..." She couldn't believe her own ears and stopped, her mouth hanging open in wonder at it all again. She was able to spit out... "You can't be serious?"

"I'm quite serious... but it won't be like that for long. And don't be silly, magic doesn't work like that. You have no reason to fly that carpet, and we have no purpose to make a gold coin. And Cookie-Jar is perfectly fine. I take her to the vet now... the wand is useless to me. Honestly Maddison." He finished with a tone just short of scolding, more along the lines of amusement. He wasn't sure how this part had escaped her until just now.

The Professor slowed his own mind and thought a bit more about the situation and how they all might be reacting to all the news that he just hadn't told them because there was no reason to.

He used a calm voice to speak to them all: "Once we have the book of words, you will learn the rest of the story about all that and a great deal more."

Maddison was certainly not calm like her Grampa had become. She exclaimed with even more anguish in her voice, "Wait... there's more... I am... this is... they are... I..."

Her mom touched her shoulder again, and this time she held it there while she spoke from behind very coolly.

"This is magic, whose season has passed. I think the Teacher is saying that it's time to renew magic."

"Is that right, Professor?" Michael asked quite seriously. "Is it time?"

"What are we talking about?... You all look so serious. Grampa, what's going on?" Maddison asked in a somewhat calmer voice, maybe coming to an understanding that this is important to hear.

Grampa began by saying, "All the items... they are history now. They belong at *The Crown* as the antiques they are. They are, already, recorded in whimsical stories, fairy tales, and great literary works so that everyone can read some version of them in some story that hints at the truth. Relics from another era... but you have special knowledge of what they actually did. You've heard what happens when we abuse the gifts that we are given."

He finished by saying, once they were eye-to-eye, and he could tell she was listening, "Those are stories worth knowing as we renew magic, Maddison. Quite possibly the most valuable understanding of what magic means."

"So, you just turn off magic? Just like that." Maddison asked.

"Oh, heavens no... Magic is here to stay. Perhaps I used the wrong words. All we do is close the book on these things... and we renew magic by believing in it once again as it was intended. You've already begun. I see you sitting silently most mornings, watching the sun rise. It's quite powerful, isn't it? So, we begin to learn and then we share. That's how you spread the truth about magic as it was intended."

Mom brought the catalog over to the Teacher and handed it to him. He thumbed through it, and they both affirmed that everything had been accounted for – everything.

They set the book down together, and she handed him a pen. He noticed that it was his pen. The pen he only took out for focused work. He smiled fondly as he took hold of it for the most focused work it would ever complete.

He signed the book, and his pen vanished just as all the people had at the beginning. The memory of him sitting with Minnie letting her know their job was to wait. To wait for this moment.

He closed the book, and the book vanished just as the pen had. Also, much like the day he blew out his everlasting candle, this room became a bit brighter once the book vanished.

It seemed like a somber moment, but they found things to talk about as they left the kitchen and headed into the big room. They sat for a while and discussed a great many things around the news they had just heard and what it would mean to have all these things at 'The Crown'.

****

Somewhere in the discussion, the Professor left the room to go back to the kitchen. Shortly before the guests arrived, he reemerged from the kitchen with a new cake. A large, round, white-frosted, Red Velvet cake. He had been working on the perfect recipe for quite some time. He admitted to them that a very attractive lady offered him a sample at the open-air market the prior fall and he fell in love with it. The way he explained the encounter to them, however, made everyone wonder with whom he had fallen in love: The cake or the *very attractive lady* as he described her.

Before anyone had the courage to go any further with that topic, the guests joined them, and the discussion shifted.

"The Curators have arrived!" He exclaimed with great excitement. "I have just brought out a cake for all of us to celebrate your new roles! Tell us! How does it feel to leave the world of Princes and Princesses to join the world as a curator for the most notable museum in the world?"

"Well, we will still raise our children as the Princes and Princesses they are. That's where the real magic is... isn't it, Professor?" The Prince asked. The Princess was already off chatting with Maddison privately.

The Prince handed a rather unique looking book to the Professor who was simply just smiling having heard from the Prince what he just heard him say.

The book was parchment white with no words on the outside. He wasn't handling it in any particular careful way. Nor did the Professor when he took hold of it. Clearly it was not in disarray for something so old... And it appeared to the Professor to be in very same condition it was while he was watching it being written. And it seemed to even have the same leather strap around it as when he knew Ambrose to tuck it away in his things for safekeeping within the royal family.

He called for the Princess, interrupting her conversation with Maddison. When she came over, the

Professor hugged her and her brother and whispered to them, "Your family is blessed. Your promises and your commitment have served you well, and you have my thanks."

The hug was neither formal or long. It was genuine and when it broke, the Princess simply said – "May I?"

The Professor handed the book to her.

The Princess sat and motioned Maddison to sit near her. Everyone else gave them some room... but Maddison grabbed her mom's hand, and they, together, sat across from the Princess.

Speaking to Maddison directly, the Princess said, "This is the book of words my family has protected since the day your mother forgave King Ambrose, the first King of Great Britain. It is that forgiveness that has sustained our family from then on and given us our purpose. Our purpose has changed now Maddison. The book is safe where it belongs."

Maddison took the book as it was offered to her. Maddison looked at the front cover, where she read, clear as day: *A love story,* but recalled at the same time that her Grampa had said it had no title.

The Princess looked at Maddison's mother, who was already reaching for the Princesses' hand. She spoke softly, but her words were something the twins would remember for the rest of their lives. She simply said, warmly, "The forgiveness was for me to heal. He simply became the man he was meant to be, thankfully."

The Professor spoke loud enough for everyone to hear him from where he was, but he was speaking to

Maddison: "Your father wrote the meaning behind all the magic we just closed the book on. The magic remains. Those items are no longer necessary, and his heart is in this book so you can understand what true magic is."

And since sentimental was *not* what the Professor was all about and there was business to tend to and cake to eat, he completely broke the mood and said for all to hear:

"Right then." Speaking to the Prince and Princess Curators, "Have your team go have a look at the study. There're just a couple things in there I won't be donating. I will take care of those shortly."

Then, turning his attention to Maddison, he said, "Maddison, I know you are heading away on holiday for a couple weeks with your mom. Take the book with you. It belongs to the two of you, of course. Read it and enjoy it. When you get back, I have something I want to show you."

The Professor then turned to Michael, speaking even louder as some of the crew walked through the room towards the study, and said, "And Michael, go grab the wand one last time, please... I will use it to conjure up a bunch more cake and a giant meal for everyone!"

Everyone stopped dead in their tracks and looked at him, not exactly sure what to say, do, or think.

The Professor secretly laughed inside at his little joke but tried to remain serious. He said to everyone who looked a little frightened, "I'm kidding. Come on... we just closed the book on this stuff... follow along. I used a double oven for three more cakes that have all been cooling. I will just go frost them now if that's ok." And he turned toward the kitchen, finally letting his face smile. He did enjoy a good prank from time to time.

Just as he was about out of the room, he hollered, "But Michael, seriously, can you help make some more coffee for everyone, please?"

Scene 15 | all the words

2020 | Midyear

The Professor breathed a sigh of what he would describe as relief. No one was in the room to hear him, but that's how he felt when he released his lungs full of air and walked into his bright study. It was the brightest it had been since... well, since it was last empty like it was on this day. It was a new feeling for him, however. It was new in the sense that what happened next wasn't entirely clear... just like when he walked into the room to wait for Maddison's father at the start, oh so long ago. He wasn't sure what he was going to say either.

And although he didn't know this is how it would eventually be renewed, he was certain it would be. And along the way, he knew that while most would trust him, he would lose some. He would have his heart burst from joy and break from sorrow. He knew the pendulum represented a powerful thing and a powerful force. To push it back the other way, good people had to do monumental work at all the right times. He felt a certain honor in being part of such a big family and doing that work from time to time.

It was refreshing to see the tea and instant coffee service tray ready to be put to work again. It was refreshing to see the empty room except for his bag of rocks and the crown on the table.

Maddison came in with her hands up, showing her Grampa her phone. The calendar was a bright lime green.

"That's my birthday color, Gramps!" She exclaimed very excitedly.

"Yes!! Happy birthday, indeed. Sixteen. You are quite the young lady if I do say so myself! Your mother and I have made a cake. I've invited a few people over. I know you have invited some of your friends from school as well. Chantel is on her way. And that party gets started when you walk in, so I wonder if I can just grab your attention for a moment. I have a gift for you too. But it's not really a party game to show around."

"You will have to forgive me, actually." He continued. "I'm sort of regifting. Actually, that's not quite right. I'm giving the same gift I have given before. Maybe that's the right way to say it."

Just then Maddison's mom joined them.

"There you are..." she said, "some of your friends are already here. More are on their way. Whatever you two are up to will have to wait."

"It'll just take a second; Grampa has a gift for me here first..." Maddison replied.

"You should join us too, dear," he said to Maddison's mom. "It will only take a moment."

He turned his attention to Maddison while her mom came behind and put her hands on her shoulders. He said, "It was in this very room before there was a castle around it that I shared some words with your dad on his sixteenth birthday. He had been my student since he was thirteen, just like you. I'd like to share them with you, Maddison, if you will let me."

She just nodded pleasantly. Inside, she was excited and wouldn't have been able to explain why if someone asked her. She was almost giddy, as evidenced by her smiling and nodding for him to continue.

She heard her Grampa say, "Some words are meant for speaking life. Some words are meant for living life."

He turned his attention to a leather bag on the table, and once it was in his hands, he continued, "I've kept track of which is which with these rocks. Before there were books, before there were scrolls or pens or anything like that... I kept the most important words I saw happening in the world on these rocks."

"They help me tell the story of what real magic makes up life itself." Grampa said.

He continued, "Would you like to resume *story time* every once in a while, and I can tell you all the words?"

He emptied the bag of rocks on his desk as if he were a child showing off his prized possessions.

All The Stories | MAGIC

- As with all tales of magic, there are great battles.

All the Stories *(Scene 13 expanded from Book 1)*

- Renewing magic to unveil the true wonders and beauty has many tales. Power, time, and human nature all seem to go to great lengths to remove the wonder and beauty.

- This story is about a collection of people who dedicated their lives to renewing magic that had been originally provided as a gift but then abused and brought to the brink of ruin over time in the hands of a very few.

In this book, we are told a handful of stories where magic is at its most abused and good people are dedicated to renewing that very magic so it can be enjoyed by all, as intended.